WET DREAMS ON LOCKDOWN

The Counselor

PARIS IMAN

URBAN AINT DEAD

URBAN AINT DEAD

P.O Box 448
Maybrook, NY 12543

Contact Author on FB: Paris Iman / IG: @authorparisiman

Contact Publisher at www.urbanaintdead.com

Email: urbanaintdead@gmail.com

ISBN: 979-8-9902387-4-9

SOUNDTRACKS

Scan the QR Code below to listen to the Soundtracks/Singles of some of your favorite U.A.D titles:

Don't have Spotify or Apple Music?
No Sweat!
Visit your choice streaming platform and search URBAN AINT DEAD.

Currently on lock serving a bid?
JPay, iHeartRadio, WHATEVER!
We got you covered.

Simply log into your facility's kiosk or tablet, go to music and
search URBAN AINT DEAD.

URBAN AINT DEAD

Like & Follow us on social media:

FB - URBAN AINT DEAD

IG: @urbanaintdead

Tik Tok - @urbanaintdead

DO NOT send original manuscript. Must be a duplicate.
Provide your synopsis and a cover letter containing your full contact information.
Thanks for considering URBAN AINT DEAD.

INTRODUCTION

FOUR YEARS EARLIER

The air was temperate with a cool breeze. The stars befrilled the dark blue blanket of the night with their ethereal glow. The stillness of the night allowed the sounds of nature to be heard more clearly.

"Damn, for somebody that just graduated with honors and got a bunch of scholarships and shit, your face sure is twisted up." Kalei joked, attempting to lighten the mood.

Isla sat in the passenger seat with her arms folded tightly. She poked her bottom lip out and allowed her chest to heave up and down.

Isla sunk into Kalei's leather seats. She often wondered where Kalei got the money to afford the brand new, 2018 Infiniti Q50. The interior and exterior were not typical.

"I don't know why you won't just come with me, Kalei!" Isla whined as she shouted in frustration.

Kalei shook his head. "I got retirement on my mind, Isla, but I also got trigger happy colleagues and the police on my back." He pulled his blunt and inhaled deeply.

"Why risk everything for drugs and all this street shit?" Isla sassed him.

Kalei maintained his composure and kept a cool head. He sighed long and hard before he replied. "Isla, I been on the streets since a jit, been hustling ever since. You know this." He paused to pass her the blunt, but she refused.

Learning to accept one another from a very young age ultimately created the most balanced relationship between them both. It was the comfort Isla felt while sitting in the same room with Kalei, in pure silence, yet they both knew how the other was feeling. It was Kalei knowing that, at the end of the day, he would always be able to call Isla for support.

All through their childhood, they worked through the pain. Growing up caused them to grow closer than ever. There was something unique about the way they were able to understand each other. From the time they were placed in the system, they had been each other's collaborators, conspirators, role models, and cautionary tales. They taught one another how to resolve conflicts and how not to, how to form friendships and when to walk away. Isla taught Kalei about the mysteries of girls, while he informed her on the puzzle of boys.

"WE!" She corrected him. "We in this shit together, been

in this shit together, and you telling me you not leaving with me?" Her voice cracked.

"I can't right now," Kalei whispered, lowering his head.

In his world, being a drug dealer was exhilarating. He found himself being able to build through hard work and determination. The things he saw, the people he encountered, and the life he now led had little foundation. The risks were immense, but the rewards, in his eyes, were even greater. He had reached a point where he couldn't turn back, and he couldn't pinpoint whether it was about the money or if it had been the rush.

The most important aspect he felt he gained had been preparation. He was equipped to handle situations that took others years to prepare for. However, more than anything, the drugs taught him to believe in himself and what he was capable of. Dealing taught him to trust his instincts and learn how to make difficult decisions.

Isla glanced back and forth in her mirrors. The light that beamed from the black truck was blinding. As it crept closer, Kalei peeped in his mirror but quickly focused his attention back on Isla. Once in eyesight, the truck came to a halt. The driver put the car in park, and Dean revealed himself from behind the tinted glass.

"What's good, Boss?" Kalei cracked his window, now giving Dean his undivided attention.

Dean's low eyes and raspy voice sent chills down Isla's spine. She squinted her eyes, so she could get a better view.

Dean had a scar that ran across his face, but he was still somewhat handsome for an old man. His brown eyes were both glossy and dreamy. His goatee was twice as long and thicker than Kalei's, and his lips were the color purple. A bed of low-cut, curly hair lie on top of his head; she couldn't pinpoint his ethnicity.

Taking a strong pull from his blunt, silence filled the air as he took his sweet time. "Go to the spot and keep an eye on that nigga, Ty, for me."

Kalei nodded his head in approval. "Got you."

Dean smirked. Leaning up in his seat, he shot Isla a piercing glare before the driver slowly drove off.

Her palms got sweaty, and her heart rate increased slightly, causing her to feel a flutter in her stomach.

Dean was the man who made both dreams and nightmares come true. He was a ruthless killer who ran Southeast with an iron fist. Dean was known for busting his guns with no conscious, quick to draw and quicker to blast a motherfucker. He was one of the most fearful and powerful men in The District. He painted the south red in more ways than one and continued to exert his influence. Back in the day, Dean made himself a multimillionaire by the tender age of twenty-one. Barely out of his teens, he built himself a reputation as one of the wealthiest kingpins to come out of The District. Dean's operation grossed $250,000 a week. He carved out an empire and flooded the streets of DC with nothing less than high quality drugs.

"I don't know what I'm going to do without you." Ignoring Dean's interruption, Isla allowed the mascara infused tears to run down her cheeks as she silently sobbed.

"Isla, I'm not goin nowhere. I'm goin always be here." Kalei assured her. He pulled his blunt once more before cutting his engine. "Go inside. I'll hit you later when I'm on my way back," he demanded.

Isla snapped her neck and flashed a slight smile. "You stayin the night?"

"Yeah, girl, I'm stayin with you. Why would I not spend my last days with you before you head to college with all of them nerdy folks?" He joked.

Isla wiped her tear-stained face, and they laughed in unison. She jumped out of Kalei's whip and watched him ride off into the night.

As she stood there, a sweep of sadness fell over her. She worried constantly about the change in the relationship between her and Kalei. The unknown rocked her world.

With her chin touching her chest and face still balled up, she trudged down the sidewalk to her front steps.

"Almost done with this shit," Isla whispered under her breath. Slowly sticking the key in the door, she sighed loudly as she entered. *Kalei need to hurry the fuck back,* she thought to herself.

"Oh, so you graduate and get some lil scholarships and think you all that, huh? Little bitch! Coming up in my house at any time of the night!" Moe spat.

As a child, because Isla didn't understand why her relationship with Moe was so tense, she was left in the dark, bewildered, unsupported, and emotionally abandoned. Today though, she could finally acknowledge Moe's envy and accept her limitations. Isla decided to stop blaming herself for the tension.

Isla quickly eyeballed the time on her phone, plagued with confusion. *It's 10 p.m. Is this bitch serious right now?*

Moe was abusive, controlling, and manipulative. She was a self-serving mother with very little inherent nurturing instinct. She subjected all of the children she took in to abuse whether it was name calling, violent rages, insensitivity, or extreme vanity. All in all, Moe was very phony and often put on a pleasant public facade.

"Oh, what, you ain't got nothing to say, huh?" she mumbled. She drunkenly paced the foyer, taking turns throwing the bottle of vodka back. "And I seen you out there with Kalei ass. Ripping and running the streets, his ass goin end up dead or in jail. And you running behind after him, your ass goin be right there, huh?" she slurred, shrugging her shoulders. "I don't give a damn. They paid me good for y'all asses."

"We look like meal tickets to you, Moe?" Isla stood in place, puzzled.

Moe burst into laughter. "Damn sure good ones." She cracked jokes.

From the time Isla was handed over to her, there wasn't a

day Isla could remember Moe being sober. It simply wasn't in her agenda.

"You disgust me. Move." Isla attempted to push past her, but Moe blocked her way. "You know, you really look a fuckin mess. Let that alcohol fuck you up like that." Isla looked her up and down.

Moe's hair had been matted to her head like a messy bird's nest. Her lips peeled and cracked from the dehydration. The only liquid she seemed to consume had been liquor; she couldn't help herself. Her big toes dangled from her slippers, and the back of her heel hung off. The jean jeggings clung to her bottom half, showing off her cellulite and clumps of fat. The droopy tank top was covered in both sweat and food droppings.

"Little girl, fuck you!" Moe whispered, and Isla could smell the stench of vodka. Her nostrils burned. "You got some balls today. Who put that battery in your back, huh? Kalei?"

Isla shrugged her shoulders and nodded her head. "You're such a cop out. By all means, enjoy a glass of something nice and have a laugh, but the inebriation is cowardly. You checked out when you had foster kids that needed you to check in," Isla expressed sincerely. "That shit robbed you of your dreams." Isla pointed to the half empty bottle of vodka Moe showcased. "You could have followed your passion, became so much more. But instead, all you did was rot your brain."

Moe scoffed and rolled her eyes. "And who the fuck do you think you are to tell me about myself, huh? I took all you ungrateful little motherfuckers in, and this is how you talk to me?"

Moe despised Isla; she hated everything about her. Isla's dark brown hair fell down her back, touching her crack. Her bronze skin glistened for no reason. Her face was clean and free of marks, pimples, and zits. Because she was all natural, Isla's nail beds were healthy while she made sure she kept her own feet done. She didn't dress inappropriately and never came off raunchy. She moved with grace and class, something Moe couldn't relate to. Isla was shapely, and her curves stuck out, especially her lower half. She had a coke bottle shape that both men and women gawked over.

Isla shook her head and slowly took a few deep breaths. "Lady, you're delusional. Now out my way." Isla pushed past her forcefully, causing Moe to slightly stumble.

"Bitch think she some kind of scholar, ole smarty pants. Ain't goin make it too far fuckin with Kalei gang bangin ass," Moe mumbled under her breath with slurred speech but loud enough for Isla to catch.

Because Isla was constantly in the spotlight, Moe didn't feel pride and joy like most parents. Instead, she felt sadness and resentment, simply because she didn't have the opportunity to shine. Moe hated Isla, and her jealously showed in the worst way. From Isla's looks, her youth, material possessions she worked for, accomplishments, and education, Moe envied it all.

The liquor took over Moe and left a fool to run her life.

She was never sober and lived in her primitive brain, which made her act accordingly. She lived in a cage.

The inside of the home was a decent size with the exception of the filth. Moe left empty bottles of alcohol scattered across the floors. The furniture was either covered in food crumbs from the children or strewn with clothing. The home had a natural stench to it, a pungent smell. The decor was mediocre and added no style to either room in the house. Isla staggered through the mess, making her way to the stairs, so she could escape to her sanctuary.

"Hey, Isla," Kannin whispered down the hall.

Isla snapped her neck in his direction. Peeping down the hall, she quickly waved for him to come. Kannin dashed down the hall and leaped into Isla's arms.

"Ouuuu, you're getting so big on me now." Isla laughed with the child before she released him. "You need to get ready for bed. School tomorrow, chump."

Kannin sulked. "I know. I know. I don't wanna go though, Isla. Have you talked to my brother?" Isla looked into his eyes and could sense they were both feeling the same pain.

Kannin was Kalei's little brother. He was tall for a twelve-year-old his age. Kannin favored Kalei in so many ways — their features were almost identical — with the exception of the fact that Kalei was much bigger in stature. They both had rich, dark skin, almond shaped eyes, button noses, and plump lips. All he needed was a fade to match Kalei's cut.

"Yes, and he said he loves you very much, and he will be coming to get you soon." She lied.

Kannin's eyes shot open, and his mouth dropped. "Really?" he whispered lightly before jumping into Isla's arms once more. "I love you guys so much." He smiled from ear to ear.

"We love you so much more, squirt. Now go get in bed before Mommy Dearest makes her presence known." Isla brought him in for a kiss on the cheek and watched him scurry down the hall back to his room.

Isla sighed deeply before she twisted the knob and flung her door open. She entered with another deep sigh of relief. The one place in the house that she adored, she got to call it her own. The room wasn't the biggest, but she made it work for her. She painted her walls turquois a few months back, and she marveled at the color. While she still held onto her twin-size sleeper, the silk bedding she applied was to die for. She had been sleeping like a princess the past few nights. The decor was minimal but chic and not too much. An accent rug lie at the foot of her bed, and two portraits hung on opposite sides of the wall. She stored her shoes both under her bed and on a rack placed on the back of her closet door which housed all of her garments. The floor lamp that adjusted with different lightings was her favorite; it always set the mood.

Isla slammed her door shut and locked it behind her. She stepped out of her clothing where she stood and stretched across her bed. She lie there in deep thought.

As she pondered on the last eighteen years of her life, it

was all a mixture of good and bad experiences. However, the most difficult part was always trying to figure out what would her fate be. She was always left with a sense of uncertainty and confusion. Being an orphan brought on extra challenges, anxiety, and fear. Moe fostered children for the wrong reasons, mainly extra money. She used it to pay rent, go on vacations, buy new frivolous items, and the rest went to her addiction: alcohol. Growing up with Moe was painful and traumatic, not just for Isla and Kalei but all of the children she took in. Moe struggled with mental health issues and addiction. Not to mention, she didn't value herself much, let alone the children she fostered.

Ty immediately grabbed Yale's ass with a rough grip and squeezed, just how she liked it. She swiveled on her own free will and stuck her ass out while reaching for Ty's cock. She caressed him, moaning softly. Ty didn't hesitate to undress himself and Yale in the process. She shoved Ty onto the naked mattress, spit in her hand, and began jerking him off, right before giving him the sloppiest blow job ever. She deep throated him while caressing his balls. Ty was in ecstasy from the way Yale sucked him up. She removed her lips and straddled him. Ty slid himself in instantly. Yale started riding him, bouncing in a particular way. He couldn't take his eyes off of her. She began to grab her tits, and she bounced up and down as hard as she could. But she allowed him the chance to hold his load for extra fun. Without warning, Ty flipped Yale onto her back and threw her legs across his shoulders. She spread her legs and invited him in. Ty shoved himself inside her and pounded away. Yale moaned loudly and hugged him tightly.

The Southside was Yale's home. She had been ripping and running the streets since a youngin'. Yale was Draco's long-time girlfriend. They had been on and off for years. Yale never wanted for anything. Draco had it all — slow money and fast money. Draco was Dean's nephew, so he was born hood royalty; popular and popping, the name rang bells. With Draco in her corner, Yale always had the benefit of getting her way in every aspect.

Her only downfall had been that she simply was a gold-digger and wanted to be with whoever was up at the time, and that hadn't been Draco. According to the streets, he was sentenced to life for a double homicide that took place months prior. Yale put on the facade as if she was staying down, playing the typical wifey roll, but behind closed doors, Ty was beating on her like a drum.

Yale was one to disguise her intentions through layers of manipulation. She was the kind of girl who would make you take her to the most expensive restaurant; she often had an impressive list of ex-boyfriends, and the men she marked were usually rich. She also had a thing for humble bragging to make herself seem less materialistic than she truly was. Nevertheless, Draco had mad love for her.

"Kalei on his way," Ty stated causally. Yale popped up and moved frantically around the somewhat empty room, collecting her belongings.

S*hit, shit, shit.* She cursed to herself. *Kalei cannot find me in here with this nigga.*

Yale jumped into her jeans and threw her tank over her head in a hurry.

"Damn, you in a rush." Ty joked as he lollygagged and took his sweet time dressing himself.

"Nigga, I ain't got time for your shit." She rolled her eyes and continued to gather her things. She snatched up her under-garments, that she forgot to put back on, and stuck them in her bag. She took one last look around the room before she headed for the front door.

"Damn, bye!" Ty shouted from the back of the room as Yale made her exit.

Kalei parallel parked a block from their usual spot. *Fuck she doin here?* he thought to himself as he squinted his eyes to make sure he got a good look at Yale. She seemed to be in a rush, and her appearance was disgruntled. Kalei closed his door and eased down the street.

Kalei's skin was so dark that he blended in with the night sky with his complexion being damn near midnight. His almond shaped eyes squinted as he observed his surroundings. Often licking his lips, he ran his hands through his goatee unknowingly. Kalei was tall and slim, but he was fit. Not too muscular, but he was tight in all the right places. The fresh fade he rocked was obvious due to the white lines that sat on the perimeter. His crisp white tee was hard to miss, especially since he was always one to sport a pair of 990s and dark navy-blue jeans.

With her head down, she rummaged through her bag as she scurried down the sidewalk.

"Sup, Yale?" Kalei stood in place. He crossed his arms and raised an eyebrow, as if he was waiting for an explanation.

Startled, Yale jumped and dropped her belongings. "Kalei, wassup, bro? I was just coming to grab some weed." She lied as she collected the contents that fell from her bag.

"Why you ain't hit me up?" he asked her with a wrinkled eyebrow. "You hit me up any other time."

Yale rolled her eyes and sucked her teeth. "Bro, do not be like that. I was in a rush, and I just stopped by." She kept her lies up as they stood in silence, grilling one another. "But, like I said, I'm in a rush. I'll holla at you." She dismissed herself in a hurry. When Kalei looked back, Yale had disappeared.

For as long as Kalei had known Yale, she was Draco's ride or die. He couldn't fathom her being disloyal, but something about their interaction threw him off.

"Something ain't right," he said under his breath as he entered the trap.

Junkies lingered in the front of the building, and hoes traded sex for drugs on the steps. Kalei scurried his way into the rundown trap house to chop it up with Ty. They ran business on the top floor of the building. Kalei, impatient, took the steps. Out of breath, he reached the door and pushed it open. The smell of used condoms filled his nostrils, and he knew. He observed his surroundings and found nothing out of place, so he left good enough alone. He paced the empty unit and found a spot on the island near the kitchen.

Entering, he was met by Ty, shirtless and out of breath as well.

"Wassup, bruh?" Ty pulled a wife beater over his head and quickly buckled his pants.

Kalei sucked his teeth and shook his head in disappointment. "Bruh, I know you did not just fuck Yale."

Ty smirked and waved Kalei off. "Nigga, why would I fuck my man's girl? Let's be real." Ty lied. "She came to grab some weed and rolled out."

Ty was not the finest thing walking, but his dick game made up for his looks. His money was also a plus. Ty favored the actor Rotimi with a wide nose and thick lips. His eyebrows connected, in the center of his forehead to be exact. It was a blessing for him to be acne free as he was already unattractive. To say the least, he was fly as he could be. He always rocked the latest designer items, and his ice told the people all they needed to know.

Kalei shrugged his shoulders, sighed loudly, and hopped on the table to collect his thoughts.

Ty was your regular snitch and get wit. He ratted anybody out to make his way to the top. While he was originally from

Southeast, his mother raised him in the suburbs and sheltered him. Now here he was, putting on a front, trying to be somebody he was not. He wanted nothing more than to be thrust into the dark, gritty underworld of the drug game, but he also wanted to be a part of Dean's in crowd. They had money, power, and respect; that was his motive.

Draco, Ty, and Kalei had been the best of friends since grade school. When Ty moved out the city, he still stayed in touch as much as he could, but the bond between Kalei and Draco was incomparable. Now that Draco was out of the picture, Ty tried to fill his place, but Kalei wasn't feeling it. As they grew older, the friendship changed drastically, but the love still remained the same to a certain extent.

"Bruh, what the fuck is up with you, my nigga? We out here getting the most money we done ever made, and your ass is sitting over there with your face screwed up." Ty threw his hands up. "Make it make sense, my nigga."

Kalei shook his head and thought carefully before he spoke.

"Yeah, we *making a lot of money,* bruh, but we also *making a lot of noise,* which will cause us to get hemmed up." Kalei expressed to him what had been on his mind, minus the constant thoughts of Isla lingering.

"Listen, bruh, if there is no evidence, there is no case." Ty shrugged his shoulders while cracking jokes.

Kalei shook his head and left it alone. He knew the topic

would come up again, and when it did, he was putting an end to a lot of shit. He just prayed he didn't run out of time.

At the tender age of nineteen, Kalei had made himself a boss, and it didn't get any higher than him on the street level. Kalei's job was to collect the money, make sure nobody ran off with drugs, and to keep shit running like clockwork on the streets. He was at the top of the food chain. Ty, on the other hand, stepped into Draco's shoes, also making him a key player. Ty was Kalei's eyes and ears on the streets. He picked up the dope, cut it, delivered it to whoever had been in need, got the money, and brought it back to Kalei. While he was the street soldier, Kalei maneuvered behind the scenes. On the outside looking in, Ty was the boss; no one knew Kalei existed unless you were that connected.

"Okay, so you mentioned your issue with the business. Now, what's really going on?" Ty pried. "It's Isla, ain't it? Shawty leaving on a full ride." He nodded his head in approval. "That's iight, bruh."

Kalei nodded his head in unison and blushed as he thought about her scholarships. "I'm so proud of that girl, man. Especially under our circumstances, I'm just glad she made it out," Kalei confessed.

"Then why the fuck is you moping about, bruh? Help me understand," Ty asked, confused.

"I love that girl, man," Kalei explained. "We grew up together and been together our entire lives. She knows me inside and out."

"Damn, I knew y'all was close, but I ain't know y'all was all lovey dovey like that." Ty joked.

Kalei shook his head and waved him off. "Man, she wants me to come with her, and I can't right now," Kalei complained.

"Yeah, bruh, too much money you goin be missing out on," Ty added.

"But something's gotta give." Kalei sighed deeply before he stood and gathered his belongings. "I'm bout to get outta here though, bruh. Hold this shit down." Kalei dapped Ty up and made his way out the door.

Swerving in and out of lanes, Kalei pulled out his blunt and allowed his thoughts to take over. Kalei knew he was in love when everything revolved around Isla. He couldn't stop thinking about her, and some days, he even preferred to spend time with her rather than doing anything else. Kalei didn't know much about relationships, but he was sure about Isla. However, his occupation stayed in the way, and he knew that would be an issue whether he liked it or not. Like any business, he had to start from the bottom and work his way up. Now that he was at the top of the food chain, there was no turning back.

Kalei pulled three blocks down from Moe's spot and walked the rest of the way. He puffed on his blunt as he glided down the street. Because Moe had thrown him out one too many times, he left for good, leaving behind Isla and his younger brother, Kannin. Not wanting to come in contact with

Moe, he knew not to hit the front. Instead, he hopped the neighbor's fence and used their ladder to reach Moe's second story. Keeping his body centered between the side rails, Kalei maintained a three-point contact by keeping two hands and one foot on the ladder always; keeping a firm grip, he made his way up. He paused when he got to the window and lowered his head as he gazed at Isla sleeping peacefully. She looked so serene; the calmness of her tranquility captured Kalei's soul. He was mesmerized instantly by the spectacle before him. His mind entered a state of gratitude as he was filled with a sense of pure privilege. He pondered on the odds, the odds of being this lucky, to be lucky enough to have experienced Isla, the perfect female specimen in his eyes. Kalei shook himself from his thoughts and made his way in. He got his stance right and used full force to push Isla's back window up enough to slide his body through. Causing a loud thud, Isla instantly jumped from a deep slumber!

"Kalei, what the fuck?!" She grabbed her chest in shock. "You almost gave me a heart attack!" She scurried to throw on clothing, and Kalei shook his head as she scrambled like a chicken with its head cut off.

"Isla." His voice made her jump. "Relax, come here." He extended his arm, reaching for her.

She stopped what she was doing and walked right into his grasp. He squeezed her tight. While her head rested on his chest, his rested on top of hers. They rocked back and forth slowly.

"I love you, girl, forever. No matter what, I want you to go and never look back. The District ain't got shit to offer you," Kalei expressed sympathetically.

Isla's eyes watered instantly; she couldn't hold it in, no matter how hard she fought to. "Kalei, I love you more, and I'm not leaving you."

"You not." He smirked. "I just need some more time. That's all. But in the meantime…" Kalei released her from his tight grasp and pushed her body from his, so he could get a good look. Still hand in hand, he allowed Isla to do a three-sixty spin for him. Losing her virginity was like a roller-coaster; she was nervous and excited all at once, not knowing what to expect.

Wasting no time undressing himself, Isla knew tonight would be the night she gave Kalei her body. He examined her silhouette in the moonlight. It was indeed enchanting.

Both Kalei and Isla took in each other's features. Kalei examined every inch of Isla's body, eyeballing her curves. Isla took in Kalei's dark, toned body. She scanned his muscles, and her eyes roamed across his chest.

Isla wore a small thong and a thin, see-through bra. Kalei pulled her close. Gently hugging her, he kissed her neck. With ease, he reached behind her to undo the bra and allowed the straps to slide down her shoulders, rapidly exposing her beautiful breasts.

They faced one another without words. Isla swung her arms around Kalei's neck, leaning into him. She could feel the warmth on his lips, and immediately, they slightly touched. Kalei ran his hands down her back, squeezing her small waist. He pulled her even closer. Intoxicated by each other's scent, they continued to kiss, exploring tongues. Kalei took her in his arms. She was almost weightless. Lowering her with ease, he began to caress her body, planting kisses, and she sighed softly. Kalei ran his tongue over each nipple, nibbling lightly as Isla stroked his back gently. Moving downward, Kalei ran his tongue from her chest to her belly button, going around it in a circle, before he reached his cherished goal. Without any pressure, Kalei snatched the thin, lacy thong off, and Isla was free. A beautiful view, she flaunted a real shell with a pearl, slightly glistening with moisture.

Kalei grinned before showering her rosebud with passion from his lips. Isla instantly took his head into one hand with the other one gripping the silk sheets. Kalei caressed her with his tongue, going in circles, up and down. Finding her little, vulnerable pea, he fondled her passionately. Isla's moans became more frequent and slowly turned into screams. Kalei thrusted his tongue as deep as he could. The never endings of his tongue could feel the micro throbbing of Isla's flaming bosom.

Squirming to get free, Isla quickly rose his head, out of breath.

"Your turn..." she whispered.

Her sexy commanding was driving him crazy, but he did as he was told. Kalei fell onto his back.

Isla kissed him on the lips as she massaged his manhood, teasing. Making the tension even greater, it was hard for Kalei to restrain himself from an explosion. Within seconds, Isla was running her tongue over the tip of his dick. Instantly, she went down and came up, covering him with kisses. Gently sucking him up, she was giving wild pleasure. Kalei was now tense. He had no more strength. He couldn't wait any longer. He flipped her on her back without warning. She was a little surprised, but Isla didn't resist as Kalei grabbed her wrists, pressing her to the bed.

She spread her legs wide in anticipation. Her hot flesh yearned to feel him inside of her, but Kalei took his time enjoying the fact that she was completely subservient to him and his power. Kissing her slowly and passionately, he simultaneously entered her quivering flesh. Isla's lips were already on his neck, and she locked her jaw as she bit down. Kalei thrusted into her slowly. It seemed as if there was no one else in the world but them. Letting go of her wrist, he hugged her back, allowing her to slide her sharpened claws across his back. At this moment, she was the cat, and he was the ball.

Isla gently reached down, squeezing Kalei tight, guiding him into her faster, letting him know to quicken the pace. He nodded in approval and gladly complied with her desire.

There was no friction, no barriers, no feigned falsity; everything was natural. They were making love in pristine form, giving one another real pleasure. Kalei slowed his pace but went as deep as he could. He could feel Isla's vaginal contractions, and he watched, enjoying the moment of true happiness with her eyes closed.

Snatching her up, he flipped her, now on all fours. Taking her by the hips, spreading her legs a little wider, he flew into her with ease, quickening his pace. As he stroked her back, Isla howled with pleasure, clutching the long-suffering sheet in her hands. As he forcibly held her hips, Isla began to convulse, trying to catch her breath. Falling onto her stomach, she yanked away from Kalei. Confused as to where she was getting her strength from, Isla quickly turned around and straddled Kalei. Putting her hands on his chest, she began to ride. Hugging her ass, Kalei admired the way she took over. Noticing her stamina was running low, Kalei grabbed her by the hips and started pounding away frantically, waiting for his peak. Isla, with her eyes closed in pure ecstasy, moaned. Kalei squeezed his eyes shut tightly and sighed long and hard.

"Ahhh!" He cried out. His warm, thick cum filled her completely. There were no complaints. Both had been pampered with pleasure. Rolling over, they snuggled up next to each other, hot and sweaty. Isla was practically passing out while Kalei was swallowing at the pounding of his own pulse.

"You made it out, girl." Kalei kissed her neck and spooned her from behind as they shared her twin sized bed. "I'm proud of you, I'm rooting for you, and I'll always be in your corner."

"Naw, we ain't make it yet," she replied with tears in her eyes as she tried to savor the moment.

"Isla, we've survived, and we can survive just about

anything for having gone through what we did," Kalei expressed.

He pulled her in closer and held her tighter.

"Don't let me go, Kalei," she whispered, drifting off to sleep.

"We got him. We got the guy at the top of the food chain." Leo talked to himself. "He's going away for a good little while." He smirked, gently caressing the wheel.

Jake turned his nose up and looked the other way.

The street was quiet, illuminated by the soft glow of the streetlights and neon signs that flickered in the distance. The cool night air was still, and the sound of distant traffic hummed in the background. Only a few windows appeared lit from inside. Reed watched as he spotted a few rats scurrying along the roadside. The feeling of unease and danger lurked in the shadows.

It seemed as if there was a neighborhood for everyone in The District. And while the city consistently ranked as one of the best places to live in the country, it wasn't all rainbows and sunshine in Washington. Some neighborhoods weren't as great as others, such as the one they were sitting in. Woodland, Southeast, one the most notorious neighborhoods, had now become Kalei's stomping grounds.

"Why do they think they can pull one over our head?" Leo smirked and shook his head.

He had his warrant written and signed by the judge; the briefing had been done as well, so he was ready. He wasted no time in advising his squad on the details of Kalei, the description of Moe's home, and the location.

He had a hard on for Kalei and wanted him off the streets as soon as possible.

"What is your issue with this boy?" Jake asked him with one eyebrow raised. He had noticed over the past few months that Leo had developed an obsession with the case.

"Excuse me?" Leo snapped his neck and looked at him in confusion.

The case had been handed to Reed months prior. Dean was the intended target; however, he always seemed to slip through the cracks of the authorities' fingers. Because of that, they focused on the people under him, Kalei specifically. He was the closest to Dean and did the majority of his dirty work, practically his number two somewhat. It was imperative to snatch Kalei up and get him talking. Dean was big time, and their goal was to get Kalei to flip on him. For months, the department had no luck when it came to Dean or his counterparts. They always returned to the office emptyhanded without further information on the criminals.

Reed considered himself the top cop in the precinct. He did what it took to get the job done at all times and didn't care what he had to do. This case had been making a mockery of his career, and he wasn't too fond of failure when it came to his profession. He was more than determined and adamant when it came to bringing Kalei in.

He considered himself to be a real cop. He liked to hunt.

He wanted to take bad guys off the streets, and he felt that nighttime presented better opportunities. "We bout to finally get this lil nigga. That means we one step closer. This lil nigga will end up a kingpin if we don't nip this in the bud now and figure out who his boss is." He tried to persuade his partner. He twisted and turned uncomfortably in his seat.

"Whatever, man. I'm following your lead on this one." Jake rolled his eyes and nodded off.

It was 3:56 p.m. Leo's favorite time to raid was always between 0400 and 0500. He knew people would be sleeping, drunk, or less aware. For him, that meant less opportunity for violent resistance.

Tuning Jake out, he directed his focus back on to Moe's house and the target ahead. Entry teams had already been hopping out to get in place. Leo had men covering the back and the front. Once the perimeter had been secured, Leo hopped out his whip on ten, ready for the action. Although against his better judgement, Jake followed his lead and was on his heels. The warrant didn't require them to knock, so Leo gave them the say-so, and they went in at full force.

"BOOM!" Moe's front door fell from the hinges, and each officer went in.

Startled and tipsy, she was taken aback and confused. "What the fuck is this?" she shouted.

"Get down! Get on the ground!" An agent pointed his gun at her head right before he shoved her face first into the ground. Moe was cuffed while the rest of the home was secured.

"Y'all ain't even no police!" Moe slurred as she examined the clothing they wore. Dressed like a well-equipped robbing crew, they all sported black pants with ballistics vests on.

Leo sauntered his way in Moe's direction and knelt beside her. "Where is Kalei?" he whispered.

"I don't know. I put that little motherfucker out a long time ago!" Moe snapped but was honest.

Leo sighed deeply, rolling his eyes. He stood up and waited for the search to be completed.

"Bring him to me!" he shouted through clenched teeth.

A search of the home was being done systematically. They made their way upstairs instantly, and the first door they hit was Isla's.

The officers set up parameters in the hallway and kicked each door in in unison. "Get on the ground! Let me see your hands!"

"Fuck, Moe!" Kalei jumped up from the bed and was tackled to the ground before he could catch his balance.

"Kalei!" Isla sobbed. "Get off of him!" she shouted in his defense.

One officer rested his kneecap on Kalei's head while the other penned him down from behind.

"Tell the boss we got him," one officer stated.

Isla was rooted in place; her stomach began to twist, causing her breathing to change. She stared with wide eyes, as if the world was crumbling beneath her. She was just there in total paralysis without realizing it.

Kalei and Isla locked eyes momentarily. "I love you," he mouthed to her right before they dragged him out.

"Kalei!" Kannin shouted from down the hall. Isla's heart sank, as did Kalei's. He turned to face his baby brother and winked at him right before dropping his head. He was led out the house.

Isla, her back up against the wall, hit the floor without hesitation. "What the fuck? Can't catch a break," she cried out loudly.

The word pain didn't do her feelings any justice. There was no single word that could encompass all of her emotions and the raw intensity behind them. Both Isla and Kalei had been to the depths of hell and back, yet nothing really hurt as bad as this. It was as if her heart had been torn, not crushed, not shattered, but torn.

Moe sauntered through the hallway and stopped at Isla's doorway. She eyeballed the frame where the door had been kicked off the hinges. "You know you goin' pay for all this shit before you leave, right?" Moe shook her head and cracked a smile. She produced a fresh bottle of vodka from behind her back and turned it up, taking it to the head. "I told you." She shook her pointer finger in Isla's direction. "Kalei ain't no good. Why you think I put his unruly ass out in the first place?"

"Moe, please, leave me alone," Isla whispered, rolling her eyes.

"Excuse me?" Moe rolled her neck dramatically. "I should beat your ass for sneaking that little motherfucka in my house in the first place," she sassed.

Isla stared at her in amazement, and silence filled the room; she was at a loss for words.

Isla knew she was supposed to keep going despite the fact that a part of her was now missing. She began to turn pale as her eyes widened. She kept her mouth shut. Instead, she lowered her head and tuned Moe out.

Chapter 1

(PRESENT DAY)

Them DC boys had the female officers going crazy. It was totally normal to walk past a cell and catch an inmate fucking an officer doggystyle or on the bottom bunk with her legs in the air. There was never a day an officer hadn't been in a cell on her knees with her head bobbing. Often times, they liked to solicit in exchange for money. One officer who happened to be an ex-stripper gave inmates dances in their cells on the regular, and they were allowed to touch, grabbing ass and tits like they were back in society.

There was no introduction at all, no small talk. Kalei lifted Brooke from the floor, pressing her against the wall. Her legs instinctively enveloped his waist, opening up her secret wet desire to his manhood bulging beneath his gym shorts. Her breasts were both big and beautiful, perfect for sucking and fucking. She offered them to him without hesitation, and he willingly attacked. Kalei allowed his teeth to rake over her erect nipples, eliciting soft moans from her lips. Kalei sucked voraciously, pressing his face into her soft flesh until he could no longer breathe. Releasing her, she touched the floor.

Brooke tugged at the waistband on his shorts, pulling them down. Kalei was swollen, like a tent pole. Brooke wrapped her hands tightly around him with both hands. She began a jacking motion, moving up and down slowly. His engorged tool now stared her in the face. She placed one hand on his balls and kept the other around his shaft. Brooke looked up and smiled as Kalei flinched from her tongue ring and the tingling sensation he felt as her hot breath warmed his balls. Her tongue, followed by her lips, on his sack made him go crazy.

Brooke's little mouth changed positions. Sucking at the head, she caught his salty precum as he was now oozing for her. Lapping the sweet spot just below the head was driving him insane as it became more sensitive, but she wouldn't dare stop. It was the sweetest, torturous pleasure.

She slid completely down until she came to a halt. He was covered in her warm saliva as Brooke's hollow cheeks intently focused on sucking the cum from his balls.

Kalei moaned, and she echoed it. He occupied a fistful of her hair, thrusting himself fully into her mouth without warning. He growled as she pushed herself onto his engorged shaft.

Feeling the back of her throat, he groaned. The tightness drove him crazy. Abandoning his thoughts, he began to wildly fuck her face. Feeling his midsection tighten, the head of his cock swelled buried deep in her throat. Brooke could feel him swelling as she watched him throw his head back and release his hot load into her sweet mouth. Kalei felt her swallowing his cum before she was done completely.

Kalei busted his nut in no time. "Damn, I guess I did need that," he whispered under his breath, shaking his head. He slowly retrieved his boxers.

"I'll see you next time. Gotta go make my rounds." Brooke winked at him while she re-dressed herself. She fixed her uniform and stepped out of Kalei's cell as if nothing ever happened.

Kalei stood to peep through the glass on his door. He scanned Brooke with his eyes as she rounded the pod. *That bitch is a problem*, he thought to himself.

Kalei re-dressed himself and got comfortable as he pondered on his time in. Being sent away hardened him and made him resistant. But it also gave him PTSD and a chip on his shoulder. He knew the institution was designed to humiliate him and diminish him in a myriad of ways, but he still pushed forward. He was stripped of his humanity, reducing his self-worth, creating a feeling of helplessness for him that was tough to rebuild. But here he was at the finish line. In a few days, he'd be a free man.

Visits were done by housing units at different times on

separate days; Yale never missed a visit. She made sure to familiarize herself with the visitation schedule, dress code policy, and always arrived fifteen minutes early. She knew firsthand not to arrive late, or her visit would be canceled.

Stepping foot in the prison, she went through the metal detector and presented her photo ID to the officer at the front desk. He nodded his head once she verified her identity. Proceeding to find a locker, stuffing her phone and purse inside, she slammed it shut. In the waiting area, she spotted a seat in the front on the far end of the room. She sat, and waited, and waited some more. After twenty minutes flew by, Brooke sauntered into the visiting area with a smirk on her face before she shouted Yale's last name. She knew that was her cue to stand up and head to the door, so Brooke could wand her and pat her down once more.

"Ughhh, this bitch," Yale mumbled under her breath.

Yale and Brooke had a love-hate relationship. While they were both sleeping with the same men, it seemed as if they were in competition of some sort.

Yale knew Brooke from back in the day, not that they were from the same part of town, but Brooke simply got around.

Brooke was pale with a freckled face, but her body was out of this world. Brooke was stacked in all the right places; she had ass and titties for days and the shape of a Coke bottle. No shots, no surgery, everything was real and home grown, which made the boys go crazy. Her long, stringy, blonde hair fell down her back. Brooke was a natural beauty. She just happened to be a whore, which made her very ugly.

"Hope you got what he's expecting," Brooke whispered in Yale's ear, referring to Draco.

Yale sucked her teeth and sighed loudly. "Bitch, just mind your business, okay?"

Brooke grinned slyly before nodding her head in the direction toward the visiting room. Yale strutted down the hall. Once she entered, she quickly scanned the room and found a seat.

Yale's navy-blue jeans clung to her body as if they had been glued on. The baggy white tee made sure it hid all of her goodies. The black and white Dunks she wore were beat up. She used them for just that purpose. She never wasted time getting dolled up to visit a penitentiary. Because of the length, she struggled to get her hair into a bun that was pushed back from her face, but she made it work. A small ball sat on top of her head, enhancing her facial features. Her brown eyes were round and wide. Yale's nose was the size of a small button, and her lips mirrored the same shape of a trapezoid.

The contraband list meant nothing to her. When it came to hiding contraband on her, Yale had an extra hiding spot. Whether it was her rectum or her vagina, she was going to stash something. Back in the day, she used to travel back and forth, swallowing as many as one hundred fifty balloons and smuggling them back into the states. While it did pose a significant risk, the money was good, so she had no reason to stop.

On this good day, however, she housed fifty-four bags of heroin, prescription drugs, and money in her vagina. Yale preferred the condom method over ingesting, simply because it was safe, not because she cared.

She twisted and turned in her seat uncomfortably. "I wish this nigga hurry up," she whispered to herself, wanting to get the drugs up out of her. Patiently, Yale waited for Draco to be released into the area. It was as if she blinked a few times and he appeared.

Draco sauntered through the visiting area like he owned the place. He walked with a slight limp and tugged on his trousers as he glided. His eyes were low and glossy, and he bit his lip at the sight of Yale. He ran his hands across his face before he took his seat.

The queasiness in her stomach had subsided, and she swiped the sweat particles from her forehead, taking a deep breath. She stood and met him halfway. Both greeted one another with open arms. Draco pulled her in, lifting her from her feet. He squeezed her tight before putting her back down.

"Wassup, girl?" Draco's raspy voice sent chills down her spine.

"I miss you. I wish this was over soon. But..." Yale's voice cracked as she lowered her head.

Draco reached across the table, gently lifting her chin.

"But it's not. I got life; you know this. But it's cool. We goin be straight." Draco assured.

Yale nodded her head, teary eyed. "Yeah, how could I forget?" she sassed with sarcasm.

Draco was no stranger to the streets. Even while he was behind bars, he never missed a beat. Bitches talked, and niggas talked. It was easy for word to get to him. He wasn't surprised when he found out Yale had started doing her own thing shortly after he got booked. That wasn't a surprise to him. While she was fucking Tom, Dick, and Harry, she still seemed to remain somewhat loyal. She never missed a phone call, the money stayed flowing through his commissary regularly, and she visited as often as he wanted her to.

Draco couldn't trust her behind his back, so a relationship was out of the picture. However, they were partners in a sense; Yale always got her cut in on whatever Draco had going on. That kept her both satisfied and grateful.

But their relationship hadn't been the same since Draco got sentenced to life. Yale knew he wasn't coming home; visits became shorter, the phone calls slowed up, and letters weren't being sent anymore. It was as if it was over, and Yale felt it. While she was tricking off here and there, her heart was still with Draco, but the feelings hadn't been mutual.

Yale shook her head. "Let's get this shit over with. I'm sick of this bitch." Draco smirked and laughed but did as he was told. He waved Brooke over, and Yale stood to make her way to the restroom, following closely behind Brooke as she escorted her.

"If you could walk any faster," Yale whispered loud enough for Brooke to hear her.

Brooke shook her head and smirked. She hardly ever had anything to say to Yale, but she insisted. "Girl, shut the fuck up and give me the drugs." She swung the door open and waited for Yale to enter. "You always running your fuckin mouth. That's all you good for," she sassed.

Yale laughed hysterically. "And all you good for is a quick fuck." She shot back. "Fuckin whore."

"Bitch, please. Guess that makes two of us." Brooke waved her off. She crossed her arms, leaned on a stall, and waited.

Yale disappeared, slamming the stall door shut and locking it, as if that was enough privacy for her. *Ughh, filthy ass bathroom*, she thought to herself as she made sure not to touch anything. Dropping her pants and undergarments, slowly and carefully, she gently pulled two condoms from her vagina and one from the rectum. She quickly snatched her pants back up onto her waist and emerged from the stall.

Brooke was still resting her back against the stall on the opposite side of the room. Stuffing her hands inside plastic gloves. she held her hand out, waiting for Yale to drop the contents.

"Here, bitch." Yale tossed the drugs in her direction, and luckily Brooke caught them right before she stormed out.

Yale speed walked back into the visiting area with a full-blown attitude. She fell into the wobbly, plastic chair and crossed her arms.

Draco leaned back in his seat and grinned. "You know I appreciate you," he stated.

"If that was the case, I wouldn't be in this predicament," she sassed, rolling both her eyes and neck. "Why you don't just ask that bitch, Brooke?"

Draco dropped his head and stood up. "I ain't doin this shit witchu. I'll hit your phone. I love you, Moe." He backed away from the sturdy table, leaving Yale teary eyed with a heavy heart. Brooke smirked and grinned slyly as she watched the scene from a distance.

LIFE AS A PRISON officer was what Brooke made it. In her mind, corrections was like the ugly stepchild of law enforcement, and in The District, the pay and benefits reflected that status. She didn't receive a gun or a nice police car. Just like any other job, she had her good days, and she had her bad days, but all in all, every day Brooke was getting her rocks off. Brooke, like majority of the female correctional officers, fucked her way to the top. She was one with low self-esteem and barely knew her worth. As a pre-teen, she was raped repeatedly, causing her to grow to be addicted to sex. Brooke wore her heart on her sleeve while still feeling unworthy of love. She formed lusty connections with inmates within the prison walls and became obsessed with both sex and money.

She scurried down the hall of the east wing. She was eager to get the drugs off of her. Once she saw the break room door from her peripheral, she dashed in that direction. Tiptoeing inside, she observed her surroundings to make sure she was alone.

She sighed with relief. "Fuckkkkk!" she whispered to herself.

Brooke wasn't the police, but she was a vital link in the penal system. The majority of officers were innocent of inappropriate behavior, but there were some who didn't follow rules, Brooke for example. She did it for the extra money; she even took risks to carry favor among certain inmates. It was a serious crime with a hefty punishment, but somehow, it never mattered to her.

The facility had thousands of high-definition cameras, advanced body scanners, and real-time inmate and staff tracking devices. Pairing that with the somewhat experienced staff and K9s, it wasn't easy to get away with bringing illicit substances into the prison. But of course, Brooke found a way around it all, with help, nonetheless.

The door to the break room squeaked as Elon gently pushed it open. Smoothly, he glided inside, shutting the door behind him.

Elon adjusted the collar on his pant suit as he crept inside the room. His receding hair line made Brooke cringe. Old age was causing him to lose hair which had been in the way of his self-esteem recently. Elon's slanted eyes were piercing. He was nicknamed yuck mouth due to the hefty number of teeth that were in his mouth, along with plaque that had been building up since before time. His dark skin was rough, dry, and ashy. But his style made up for what he lacked in looks, and his sex game — that wasn't up for debate.

A combination of anxiety and dread hit her all at once.

"I hope you have it." Elon's voice traveled throughout the room. "Cause if not..."

Brooke cut him off mid-sentence. "I do. You know I do." She rolled her eyes, removing the full condoms of drugs she had just retrieved from Yale prior from underneath her uniform.

Elon was granted the Regional Director position, so he felt superior. He figured he had no boundaries, and things were to go his way or the highway. The facility was the only place he exuded confidence, and he treated the inmates and staff members the exact same.

"Always a pleasure doing business with you." He reached out for the contents, and she flung them in his direction. "You keep your mouth shut, and I do the same." He winked.

Elon was a manipulative, narcissistic asshole. He was two years older than Dean but much softer. Throughout the years, he tried his hardest to portray the tough guy act, but he just didn't have it in him. He and Dean were the complete opposite; Dean was a bad boy, while he was a good boy. While

Dean reaped the benefits of having all the bitches, money, and more, Elon found himself stuck in the shadows of his baby brother. Both had power, allies, and connections in high places, but Elon hadn't been as connected as Dean.

For weeks, Elon had been using and abusing Brooke every chance he got. He was one to enforce the rules, and once he found out that she had been giving it up to several different inmates, he used that to his advantage. Brooke had been bringing in drugs for both Kalei and Draco for months since they were housed at the facility. Elon had been taking the drugs; he either laced whatever had been brought in, or he was cutting the product. Brooke couldn't figure out his motive, but she did as she was told. The last thing she wanted to lose was her job, so she complied.

LIFE IN THE DISTRICT was still the same as she remembered it. Isla drove by, rubber necking, getting glimpses of old row homes she once knew and popular landmarks. Of course, The District didn't come without its dangers, and the crime rate was higher than high.

The south side hadn't changed. Isla watched as she passed a card game in session. Officers nearby leaned against cars, children rode their bikes, it was a sight to see. She noticed Rowdy, an old head from around her way. Rowdy wasn't a kingpin; he was simply an expletive from the hood trying to survive. He did drugs, he sold drugs, and he helped destroy his community. Now here he was, trying to save it. The scene warmed her heart. She was happy to be back.

Isla hit the corner, turning into the worst gas station on the block, but she was on E and had no choice. Fiends lined up near the door; others were scattered around the pump. The stench of hot piss invaded her nostrils when she exited her vehicle. She quickly brought her hands to her nose, balling her face up.

"Ughhhh, let me get this over with," she whispered.

Bracing herself for what she knew was to come, she pumped toward the inside to pay for her gas. All eyes were on her. Mouths dropped instantly.

While she looked the same in every aspect, she did gain a bit of weight and had grown more into her features. Isla rocked a blunt cut bob with freshly manicured feet and nails. Her brows were snatched, and her face was glowing. Cloaked in an Armani pants suit, every curve was noticeable. Perky Ds sat up on her chest, her hips spread wide and plump, and her booty jiggled when she walked. "Don't you dare lift a finger, beautiful." A junkie rushed past her to the door, swinging it open for her. "A gentleman, I am." He bowed and flashed her a smile.

Isla nodded her head, scurrying inside.

"Oh, my God, it's you," Yale shouted as she turned around to face Isla after walking in the door. Yale lunged in her direction, hugging her tight.

"Yale?" Isla asked with a puzzled look.

"Yes, bitch, it's me in the flesh." Yale turned and did a three-sixty spin for Isla.

Yale hadn't changed a bit. She was still the same loud-mouth, fake, bougie girl from high school Isla remembered. The feed-ins she rocked glistened as they were fresh. Isla could tell from her dry skin and purple lips that she had been indulging in more than she could handle. The dingy sweats, white beater, and rundown Crocs made her look slightly homeless, but Isla was never one to judge.

"Girl, you look good. What you doin back in the city? Ain't shit goin on here." Yale tucked her arms and waited for Isla's response.

Isla shrugged her shoulders. "It was time for me to come home. Home is where the heart is." She looked around, scanning her surroundings, realizing how bad she had missed everything about home. "I've become a licensed psychiatrist, and I'm done with school, so I figured why not find a job back at home, you know?" she confessed.

Yale grinned and nodded. "Isla, that's wassup. I'm happy for you. You actually got the fuck out and made something out of yourself."

Isla shook her head as she thought about her upbringing. "I had no choice; something had to give."

"Let's catch up." Yale snatched Isla's phone from her hand, storing her number after dialing herself. "I'll shoot you a text. Don't be duckin' me now." She joked.

Isla laughed and waved Yale off. She hurried to pay for her gas and was on her way.

"Oh, hell no!" Isla whispered to herself as she peeped out the window occasionally but still kept her eyes on the road. After graduation, she pushed her fears to the side, packed her bags, and headed up north. Leaving was no easy decision, but it was the best thing for her. When the mini panic attack concluded, she realized the beauty in the new move. She was opened to so much newness — from meeting new people, tasting new foods, the hustle and bustle of the new city, and simply becoming accustomed to her new life. It left her feeling amazing, but now, she was back in The District.

"Why does it look like this?" she whispered once more with wide eyes.

Washington's District had a fascinating mix, each with its own unique character. There were the trendy hipster zones, sophisticated quarters, student-friendly locales, and unfortunately, the less desirable areas like the one Isla had currently been in. Isla took note of the homeless people that scattered throughout the streets and lingered on the sidewalks. The corner boys were exposed but moved as if they were untouchable, garbage flooded the narrow streets, and a strong stench of phencyclidine polluted the air.

Moe was the last person she wanted to see, but she had no choice but to go through her to see Kannin. Throughout the years, she learned how to deal and cope with her past traumatic experiences, so she was pretty confident when it came to her maintaining her composure and not losing her shit.

The last face she wanted to see was Moe's, but she had made promises and couldn't let them go unfulfilled. It had been four long years since she had seen or heard from Kalei. His whereabouts were unknown, but she knew for a fact she could still get custody of Kannin. That was her top priority.

Isla parallel parked her BMW in front of Moe's row home. She cut the engine and threw her head back as she sighed deeply. "God, give me strength." With her eyes shut tight, she spoke to herself out loud.

Dramatically exiting the vehicle, she slowly made her way.

"Well, look who the fuck it is." Moe snarled as she swung the door open and examined Isla from head to toe. "The fuck you want? Creeping up on my porch like you all that. With your lil hair all done up nice, jewelry, and expensive high heels." She insulted her.

Moe hadn't changed personality wise, but her appearance itself was horrific. The alcohol did a number on her. Isla barely recognized the woman. Her hair had been matted to her head, a stench traveled when she spoke, and her teeth had become rotten. She had always been a bamma so getting dressed was never in her daily routine. The bottoms of her feet were black, and dirt protruded from under her toenails. She stood cloaked in a nightgown from years prior, allowing a deadly smell to linger on her.

Isla shook her head and turned her nose up. "Well, I can see ain't shit changed with you." She smirked with folded arms.

Moe hadn't changed a bit. In fact, her appearance had worsened. Moe made what was supposed to be home lonely, controlling, and ruthless while in her presence; it was a nightmare.

"Is you going to let me in or what?" Isla sassed, but Moe didn't budge from the doorway.

Instead, she looked around cluelessly. "Why I'm letting you in my house?"

"Lady, cut the shit. Let me in. I'm here for Kannin. Not you. Don't get that confused," she stated sarcastically.

Moe wobbled outside to invade Isla's space as if she wanted to intimidate her. "I put the little motherfucker out, just like his brother," she hissed.

Between her appearance and loss in coordination, Isla knew she was bent.

"Well, where can I find him?" Isla began to grow irritated.

Moe shrugged her shoulders and swayed from side to side. "I don't know, ripping and running the streets like his brother. That's all they're good for," she slurred.

Isla turned on her heels, dramatically rushing to her car. She hopped in her whip and took off without hesitation. Guilt was suffocating her, leaving a heavy feeling in her chest. She wasn't able to concentrate on any tasks at hand as it paired with shame reminding her of how she failed in the past.

Dashing down the street, nearly bending the corner, the sight of Kannin struck her by surprise. "Jesus Christ!" Isla gripped her chest. "He looks like a spitting image of Kalei. What the fuck?" she whispered to herself.

Quickly, she put her car in park and hopped out in a rush. Heads turned, and all eyes were on her as she strutted across the street in Kannin's direction. The whole hood was on the lookout, but not once did Kannin look up. As she inched closer and reached the sidewalk, she was confronted by one of Kannin's men.

He extended his arm and gently pushed her backwards. "Damn, Ma, you in a rush? You looking for somebody?" Niko asked as he eyeballed her figure and curves.

Isla placed her hand on her hip and titled her head to the side. "You got less than three seconds to get the fuck out my way." She threatened him.

Niko was tall with a slight muscular build. His skin was the complexion of coffee, but he happened to be covered in graffiti. His wide nose and full lips were not his best features, but they were the most noticeable. Niko was Kannin's muscle. Anybody got out of line, Niko was handling it. He was known for getting motherfuckers in check and, more importantly, deading those who crossed lines.

"Or what?" Niko sized her up as his facial expression changed; he invaded her space.

"Or you goin have to deal with me." Kannin's voice echoed from a short distance back.

Kannin sat back in a lawn chair. He continued to pearl the blunt he had been working on before he looked up. Locking eyes with one another, he was relieved to see Isla.

While her mind didn't seem to be going with the steady rhythm, it was juggling between the past, present, and the future thoughts. But it was a sudden wind that blew past her, wiping away all of her anxiety and stress. Instinctively, she closed her eyes. It was in that moment when she experienced the calm within her, a feeling of relief. Isla let her guard down and cracked a smile and shoved Niko to the side. She rushed Kannin instantly.

Isla figured her mind had been playing tricks on her with the way Kannin looked identical to Kalei.

He rocked a low-cut fade, and his facial hairs had begun to sprout. The white tee he sported was crisp and clean, along with the cargos he paired with it. The 990s on his feet looked as if they had just been taken out of the box. Isla was looking for his usual hyperactive greeting, but she realized he wasn't a small boy anymore. Kannin scanned the area and observed his surroundings as he approached Isla. His demeanor was subtle, and energy was calm, but he still kept his head on a swivel. He was aways paying attention and more focused than ever. The gullible, innocent child that was oblivious to all was no longer in there. "Oh, my God, my baby isn't a baby anymore." Isla joked as she poked her lip out and leaped into Kannin's arms for a hug.

He scooped her up from her feet, allowing them to dangle in the air. "Hell naw, I'm grown now."

"Oh, my God, look at you!" Isla dramatically pushed back to examine the young boy she once knew who had grown into a young man. "You literally look like a spitting image of Kalei."

"I know. I get that a lot." He shook his head as a wave of sadness came over them both.

"Where is he?" Isla questioned Kannin as she looked around.

Kannin shook his head and lit his blunt before responding. "Man, he supposed to come home this year. Real soon hopefully."

"The fuck! He still locked up?" Isla stared at Kannin blankly as he nodded his head.

Isla placed her hands back on her hips and balled her face up. "Okay, well, what's all this?" She pointed to their surroundings, referring to him being in the streets.

Kannin shrugged once more. "Picking up where bro left off, ya know? Or following in his footsteps, as Moe would call it." He smirked and shook his head.

"What the fuck even happened with you and Moe? Where are you staying?" Isla asked with a concerned look.

"Mannnnnn." Kannin took a long pull and exhaled before he began. "I was fed up with that bitch, Isla. She was fuckin nuts! Like a year or two after you left, that bitch beat me, took me outside, and put a fuckin dog collar on my neck." He paused before he began again. "Bitch cuffed me to the pole in the backyard and kept me outside overnight for a week."

"Are you serious right now, Kannin?" Isla asked, already knowing the answer. Her eyes began to water.

Kannin chuckled lightly. "Man, I beat the dog shit out her ass when she took that collar off of me. No mercy. I tore her down," he stated through clenched teeth.

"Okay, look," Isla pulled out her device from her back pocket and made Kannin store his number, "I have to go, but I'll be in touch, and when I get settled, you're coming to stay with me." She assured.

Kannin nodded and grinned before he pulled her in for a tight hug. "Love you, Isla. You all I got."

"I love you too, baby boy, forever."

ISLA FOUND herself hanging off the end of Mississippi Avenue in a newly renovated, single-family home that she had landed with a new homeowner loan. The house was approximately three thousand square feet, ideally located in the heart of the south.

Isla emerged from her whip and stood on the curb as she watched Devyn recklessly fly down the same street and parallel park behind her. She was noticed from a mile away, and you could hear her coming. She slammed on brakes and put the car in park.

"Welcome home, beautiful." She hopped out with a bright smile and open arms.

Isla laughed and shook her head. "You are really fuckin simple, you know that?" She joked. "Is you goin help me with this shit?" Isla pointed at the rest of the belongings dangling from her backseat. She looked her up and down as she watched her struggle.

Devyn burst into laughter before she sprang into action. "Damn, my bad."

Devyn was on the shorter side and slightly heavyset. Tattoos covered her vanilla-colored skin. Her hair reached her shoulders, but she often sported ponytails or rocked a fresh set of feed-ins. Devyn was very well kept and never in a million years planned on letting herself go. She stayed in the latest designer items and classified herself as a sneaker head.

Devyn and Isla met in high school and had been the best of friends since. Isla knew firsthand that Devyn identified as gay and never judged her. Never speaking on it, Isla never mentioned she was going away for college, but somehow, Devyn managed to end up at the same university. While Kalei's arrest and their splitting had her in a horrible space for months, Devyn was there to ease majority of the pain.

The open floor concept, the generous rooms, stainless steel appliances, granite kitchen, and large family room impressed her instantly. It gave her the benefit of living in the city while having the serenity of the suburbs. "This is it," Devyn cheerfully whispered as she took in the home. "How the hell you manage to buy a house and have this bitch furnished to your liking from another state?" She questioned her with a puzzled expression.

Isla smirked. "Listen, I have my ways." She strutted through the home, taking in all of her new amenities and features.

"But look though, I wanted to holla at you to see if you was interested." Devyn got her attention. "There's a position at my job that I figured was up your alley."

"Really, D? I appreciate that." Isla smiled, showing off her pearly whites.

Devyn grinned slyly. "It's for a psychiatrist position. I know you still working on getting all your certifications, but I'm sure it won't hurt for you to stop past for an interview."

Isla stood with her arms folded, contemplating on the gesture. "I guess it wouldn't hurt to give it a shot." She shrugged her shoulders.

"Yeah, it won't." Devyn assured. "Get there tomorrow at 10 a.m. Let them know you there to see the warden for an interview, and she'll be expecting you."

Isla raised her eyebrows and smirked, placing one hand on her hip. "Oh, you got you some pull, huh?" She joked.

Devyn bit her lip as she invaded Isla's space. She grabbed her waist tightly and pulled her in close.

"You done with the tour?" she asked in a low tone before their lips met. Isla nodded and allowed Devyn to plant kisses down her neck.

Good, now it's time to break this bitch in, Devyn thought to herself.

After progressively spending more and more time together, Isla and Devyn became somewhat best friends. They did damn near everything together. However, Devyn's attraction to her became stronger and stronger.

In the beginning, Devyn figured they were just close friends. But she wanted more from Isla. She denied her feelings for the longest time, but she eventually came to terms and accepted them. In her mind, she loved Isla and didn't want to do anything to jeopardize their friendship. But oftentimes, she didn't know if the feelings were mutual, but Devyn certainly gave her unintentional clues from time to time.

Devyn slid in bed next to Isla. Isla's eyes closed, and Devyn gazed at her, the most beautiful woman she'd ever seen. All she wanted to do was rip her clothing off and make love to her. Devyn's hands moved toward her pussy while Isla faked sleep. Suddenly, she turned her head and shot a piercing glare at Devyn. She said nothing as Devyn crept down her body, looking in her eyes. She roughly tugged on her panties until they were off. She used her tongue and slowly licked Isla's swollen lips while her hands massaged her buttocks.

"Ahhhhh," Isla whispered.

Her breathing increased as well as her heartrate while Devyn was still licking and sucking her lips. By this time, Isla's clit was the size of a pea. Devyn saw it and went in for the kill. Her mouth covered her clit as she used her tongue to massage and suck on it.

"Devyn, oh, my God," Isla shrieked.

That only encouraged her as she used one of her hands to finger her soaking wet pussy. Isla could hear her juices slopping each time Devyn thrusted a finger into her hole. She didn't stop; she continued to savagely fuck her pussy with her fingers.

Devyn looked into Isla's eyes as she ate her up. Waves of pleasure pulsed through her body as her orgasm hit. Devyn rubbed her clit even harder and used her other hand to finger her pussy faster until Isla's orgasm subsided.

"Damn, boo," Devyn whispered with a huge smile plastered across her face.

Isla's legs felt wobbly, but she slowly regained her breath and composure.

Chapter 2

"Kalei!" Isla's loud, high-pitched scream was filled with terror and rang out through her new home. It rattled the walls as she shouted from her chest. Covered in a cold sweat, she forcefully kicked the comforter and sheets from her naked body and watched them fall to the floor. Heart pounding, she looked around the room suspiciously before stumbling to the bathroom.

These fuckin dreams, man, she thought to herself. Isla looked in the mirror, examining herself cautiously. She flung her hair from one side to the other and began her morning routine. Taking a seat on the toilet, she reached over and hit the shower. Turning the handle back and forth, she adjusted the temperatures. The water running soothed her to a certain extent, coupled with the warm, yellow rays that struck her through the window. Dust molecules floated in the air. Isla stepped in and allowed the water to cascade down her back, absorbing the warmth like a sponge. These were the few minutes of her day where her mind was completely clear — a hiatus in her busy life. Just like the water, the shower was a diverse place. It was her go to for thinking and contemplation. It was her personal stage for her very own singing performances, and more importantly, it was the place where she felt fresh. Isla allowed her mind to go blank. Shutting her eyes tight, the sound of the water invigorated her. The first drops were cold but quickly became warm, and soon, steam filled the room and moistened her skin. Isla put on her thinking face and stared to the ceiling. Her frown became deeper, but it was mixed with a sudden relaxation, and her eyes began to twinkle at the thought of Kalei.

Reluctantly, after twenty minutes, Isla forced herself out, emerging a new woman, feeling revived, refreshed, and rejuvenated. *Sheeesh!* Isla shivered as she stepped out the bathroom. She maneuvered around the room until the conversation with Devyn dawned on her. She rushed to the end table and grabbed her phone, looking at the time. "What the fuck?! I'm going to be late," she screeched. Isla rummaged through her closet, grabbing a black pant suit and pairing it with a closed-toe pump. Isla's heels echoed throughout the home as she ran from room to room. Snatching her hair back into a ponytail, she darted back to the bathroom and sprayed herself twice. "Can't go smelling like shit, girl." She joked. Grabbing her purse and a small briefcase full of nothing, she hit the door without looking back. "Let's get this show on the road." She pumped down the hall, ready to wing it all.

ISLA APPROACHED the prison gate that stood approximately fourteen feet high, a brooding, grey mass of steel beams and mesh, topped by razor wire. There was no beauty in the design, only brutal efficiency. The only color in sight was on the warning signage; all else was bleak. The door she approached to enter was an interior door, dark grey metal, sliding in into a recess wall. It was about six inches thick, no more than eight feet tall. It was massive. Isla stared in amazement as she tried to guess how much it weighed. What made the biggest impression on her was how it sounded as it locked behind her. The facility appeared to be a four-level building, divided into eight different blocks. The blocks were designated by category, rather than alphabetically. The reception area contained a typical office reception with a height chart for the mug shots and showers nearby for all incoming inmates.

Isla nervously stumbled through the metal detectors as she was still observing her surroundings and scanning the area. "Can I help you, ma'am?" A guard shouted in her direction.

"Uhhh," Isla mumbled. "Yes, yeah, I'm here for an interview."

The guard turned his back and started pointing in different

directions. "You're gonna go down this hall, make a sharp left, and the warden should be expecting you."

Isla nodded. "Thank you." She flashed a fake smile as she reluctantly escorted herself through the facility. The dreary vibe was all consuming, as it was drab. She was instantly hit with a sense of nothingness. She examined the prison with her curiosity, wondering how many souls had passed through; she shuddered. Bending the corner and following the rest of the directions, she stopped at a big, black door with a golden knob. The heavy moans coming from behind the door caused her to pause. She hesitated and backed away. *I guess I should wait,* she thought to herself as she looked around.

Rita was wearing a white blouse and a form fitting, blue skirt that stopped just above her knee. Her choice of clothing accented her athletic form perfectly. She also possessed piercing eyes, which happened to be the most beautiful shade of brown. Her make-up and long, black hair were done to perfection as well. She was a vision of beauty.

Elon slowly leaned in to kips her lips, and she, in turn, did the same. Second by second, their kisses became faster and more passionate. Before long, both of their tongues were in search for each other's mouths recklessly.

As the fire between them grew, Elon started to unbutton and remove her blouse. Rita assisted him by removing her bra. Stunned by the heavenly sight in front of him, he firmly grabbed them and greedily sucked. Her nipples became erect instantly as he repeated the process on each breast. Reaching under her skirt to remove her panties, he grinned slyly when he realized she hadn't been wearing any.

Pleasantly surprised, he immediately pushed her back toward her desk. Rita slid on top, and Elon knelt before her, thrusting his head between her legs to lick away. She tasted delicious. She moaned quietly before her hips began to buck wildly. In no time, she orgasmed powerfully and pushed Elon to the side so that he would cease his stimulation.

He rose to his feet, removing his pants, so she could finally see how rock hard he was. Leaning in closer, he gave her a quick passionate kiss right before lifting her back onto her desk. He gently placed his aching penis inside of her, thrusting slowly. Elon let out an involuntary grunt as he marveled at the warm tightness. Wishing they could stay like this forever; they both were on the verge of an uncontrollable release. Suddenly, reaching the height of excitement at the same time, Elon pulled out and uncontrollably shot out several pools of hot jism throughout the office. Both exhausted, they blushed and laughed in unison.

Isla, embarrassed, let herself in after the loud moans ceased. She tiptoed her way into the warden's office space. Rita stood behind her desk with a smile plastered on her face as she attempted to fix her clothing.

"Good morning, Ms. Harrison, my apologies. Sorry for the delay." She moved from behind the desk and extended her hand.

Hesitantly, Isla shook it. *I have no idea what you were just doing with these hands, lady*, she thought to herself. "Nice to meet you." She accepted the gesture and nodded her head in approval, flashing a smile.

"I'm Warden Taylor, but you can call me Rita. This over here is Mr. Harris. He's the Regional Director of the facility," she explained.

Isla focused her attention on Elon. He extended his hand, but the bulge in his pants caught her off guard.

Jesus Christ, she thought to herself, making sure there wasn't much eye contact.

"You can have a seat, and we can go on and get started." Rita directed her to one of the two chairs.

"Can you tell me the difference between jail and prison?" Elon, still in the corner dressing himself, threw the first question out.

"No, no, I cannot. I've never worked within the justice system before," Isla replied honestly.

"Well, at least you're honest," Rita mumbled as she fell back in her chair and crossed her legs.

"It's cool." Elon smirked and flashed a smile in Isla's direction. Rita rolled her eyes, making a mental note. "Jails are usually local facilities under the jurisdiction of a city, local district, or county. Jails are short-term holding facilities for the newly arrested and those awaiting trial or sentencing. Those that are sentenced to serve a short amount of time are housed at a local jail. Whereas prisons are institutional facilities under the jurisdiction of the state or federal government, where convicted offenders serve longer sentences," he explained.

Isla nodded her head with wide eyes as she took in the information.

"Okay, let's get down to the nitty gritty. Where you from? What was home life like for you? Describe to me you in one word." Rita bombarded her with questions.

"Uhhh, okay. I'm from here... the city. I was an orphan, so home life for me was some shit if we're being honest," Isla stated with a blank stare, leaving Rita at a loss for words. "Me, a word... loyal."

"Tell me a little bit about your background and education." Elon pried.

"Well, I have a bachelor's degree. I completed and passed my MCAT, and I've obtained my license to practice psychiatry," Isla replied.

Rita nodded her head, collecting her thoughts. "An orphan turned psychiatrist. How'd you do it?"

"With God on my side always. It wasn't easy. I don't know my parents, and my foster mother was as worse as they come. I went to school, got good grades, and kept my head down. How'd I make it to college with no money? Oh, the scholarships did that. I just put in the work. Ultimately, I knew I was fucked up growing up. I didn't want to stay fucked up, so I got help, and in turn, I knew that was my cue. Helping others was my calling," she confessed.

"But why a psychiatrist of all things?" Rita challenged her.

Isla sighed deeply. "I have the potential to make a pretty impressive salary in this field. Not to mention, it is in demand, I have the ability to help others, and every day is different."

Elon leaned on the edge of Rita's desk and flashed another smile at Isla. "I think you'd be a good fit here. We could definitely use someone like you on the team."

Rita stood to her feet. "You've got the job, Ms. Harrison. I expect to see you tomorrow, bright eyed and bushy tailed." She flashed a fake smile before dismissing her.

Isla paused as a look of puzzlement and surprise crossed her face. Quicky shaking out of her trance, she rose to her feet and extended her hand, taking them up on the offer. "Thank you so much." Isla reached to shake their hands once more. "I will see you both tomorrow."

Once Isla was out of sight and the door was shut behind her, Rita let loose.

"What the fuck is wrong with you, E?" Rita sassed. "Listen and hear me good when I tell you, you are free to do whatever the fuck you want, just as I am free to initiate a divorce while simultaneously tapping the fidelity clause on our marriage contract."

Elon smirked as he stood in silence and shook his head. "Baby, I need you to relax."

"No, I won't. Your ass is skating on thin ice, my nigga." She stuck her pointer finger in his face. "I give you an inch, and your ass wanna take a mile."

"So, you basically saying the best and only real way to

make this work for me is to find a woman that is already into polygamy?" Elon playfully joked.

"You think everything is a fuckin joke. You can't have your cake and eat it too, Elon." Rita snapped. "Someone is going to end up extremely unhappy either way, or we can simply accept that we have different ideals. Not everyone is hardwired to be monogamous. But what I don't recommend is that we kid ourselves into believing this will be okay because it won't. It will fester into deep seeded resentment," she confessed. "So, you let that marinate before you're ready to come to me with your decision."

Elon waved her off and let her have her moment.

Like any other marriage, theirs had its ups and downs, but Elon wanted to have his cake and eat it too. Not only did he want Rita for himself, but he wanted others as well. Rita never once objected to a little fun here and there in the bedroom, but when it became repetitive, issues began to arise. She soon came to the conclusion that Elon simply wasn't satisfied with one woman. When Rita figured that he wouldn't stop, she began to step out occasionally.

Although the sex was immaculate here and there, Rita wanted out. While Elon was free to do what he wanted, she felt she was free to initiate a divorce. Either way, someone would always be unhappy. Rita didn't object to his ideals; however, it wasn't something she wanted to compromise on. Not everyone was wired for poly, and she definitely wasn't. What she wasn't going to continue doing was kidding herself into believing that she could sacrifice her own happiness and things would be okay. She began to fester deep resentment and figured the only way to deal with these issues was to let Elon go and allow him to find a woman that was into polygamy. Rita was never one known for letting a man make her be okay with something she wasn't already okay with.

Now that she had landed the job, she was on her own. *Now, how the hell I get out of this maze?* she asked herself as she maneuvered through the corridors until she reached the main gate.

"Good morning, Mr. D.," a raunchy CO shouted down the hall at Dean, causing heads to swivel, including Isla's.

Making eye contact with the man of the hour, Isla's heart sank, and she gasped for air.

Dean hadn't cracked, with the exception of the protruding grays that gave off his age. Isla had never seen him up close and personal before. In fact, she had only ever caught glimpses of him here and there. Dean was like a ghost that made appearances in the hood every so often. His eyes were low and dreamy, and he was clean shaven all around. The pant suit he sported had been tailored to perfection, and the Bond 49 scent lingered behind him as he maneuvered. She was totally taken aback as she had only ever known him to be the streets' biggest badass. To see him dressed to a T in a professional setting left her in deep thought.

Turning on her heels, she scurried through the detectors and speed walked to her car.

Just as Elon was exiting, Dean was entering.

"Jesus, give me a break." Rita looked to the ceiling and whispered to herself. She fell back in her chair and kicked her feet up.

Elon shot Dean piercing stares, but Dean never once acknowledged him. Instead, he shut the door behind him.

Rita shook her head. "I do not have time for y'all shit."

Dean sucked his teeth. "Ain't nobody thinking bout that nigga."

"He is stressin' me out," she confessed.

"Damn, sounds like a personal problem to me. Should have picked the right brother." Dean joked as he was referring to himself. "Definitely wouldn't be doing all that stressin' you doin." He eyeballed her curves.

Dean and Rita were lovers once upon a time. Dean had her first, and Elon snatched her right from up under his nose; but that was her karma. They had been the best of friends and loved one another deeply, but Dean was focused on his come up and put Rita on the back burner. The attention, the affection, everything she wanted from Dean, she found in Elon. Dean was hustling day and night to provide and make sure things were set for him in the future. At a young age, Rita didn't see the bigger picture. She didn't hesitate kicking Dean to the curb and falling for the jealous, narcissistic, worthless older brother.

Although hurt, Dean let it be and wished her the best. He vowed to always have her back and be in her corner regardless of their situation or differences. His loyalty never changed, still to this day.

In her predicament now, she looked back and wished she could turn back the hands of time. After years of failed marriage, Rita knew she made the wrong decision when she chose Elon. She pondered day and night on her mishaps and craved Dean. While she had been feigning for love, Dean was prioritizing. Now, here he was, pretty much the man in charge, and she couldn't have him.

"Dean, go straight to hell. You ain't too faithful your damn self," Rita sassed, rolling her eyes.

"Man, look, I ain't even here for all that. I need to holla at you bout one of my guys."

Dean had his hands in everything you could think of. His connections in the justice department ran deep. Always dressed in business attire, he still managed to be the boss supplying all the heavy narcotics. That was where Rita came in; everyone played an intricate role in his operation. She, however, just made sure things ran smoothly.

"Who? Mr. Kalei? You know you can't be showing favoritism. They don't like that." Rita added her input.

Dean laughed hysterically. "Ri, this shit not a game. Fuck favoritism. That's the lil nigga that's goin fill my shoes. Nigga been up under my wing since before I can remember. If you ask me, that's my son."

Rita shook her head, and silence filled the room, and she ventured down memory lane.

"I remember back in the day you used to always say you wanted a little boy."

Dean nodded as he pondered on his thoughts. "I did used to say that. I did. That's crazy I found Kalei when I did. I'm super grateful for that lil nigga."

"Where did you even find him?" Intrigued, Rita sat up and wanted the full story.

"On the street." Dean began. "Kalei was an orphan. Foster mother was some shit, but what's new? I took him in when she put him out. Unfortunately, I wasn't able to get custody of his younger brother, Kannin, but now that he's a little older, I been keeping my eyes on him, making sure he straight until Kalei touch down."

"The Grim Reaper but with a heart of gold, so genuine, the most loyal," Rita whispered, staring deep into Dean's eyes. "I love you, Dean. I always will."

"I love you too, Ri, but I ain't goin hold you up, beautiful. Just make sure my boy straight and stop letting that bitch ass nigga stress you out." He rose from his seat, invading her space. He yanked her from the seat, pulling her in for a hug. "That nigga keep playin' around, I'm goin have to make you mine again." They both laughed in unison. Dean buried his face in Rita's neck and plated a few kisses before he released his grip.

"Bye, D. I will make sure your boy is straight." Rita assured as Dean was making his way through the door. He winked at her, flashing a smile that made her drawers wet instantly.

HIGHLANDS WAS the neighborhood spot on the Southside. It was the place for family and friends to gather and enjoy themselves. Between the coffee and the food, the service and atmosphere was a ten out of ten. Highlands had become the focal point of community connection.

"Oh, my goodness!" Mrs. Juanita shouted. "Welcome home, my pretty." Her thick accent traveled throughout the restaurant.

Feeling more than welcomed, Isla charged Mrs. Juanita and pulled her in for a tight hug. She inhaled deeply, taking it all in.

"It's been so long. How are you?" Isla held back happy tears.

"I'm good, Mama. Come, have seat." Mrs. Juanita walked her to an empty table and got her started. "For one or two?"

Isla blushed and threw up her fingers, indicating that it would be two.

"Ouuuu, Kalei joining you?" Mrs. Juanita grinned hard.

Isla shook her head. "No, not today. Kannin is meeting me."

"Ohhh, okay." Mrs. Juanita poked her lip out. "I'll get you

guys food and drinks in." She waddled to the back of the kitchen, leaving Isla in deep thought.

Within seconds, Kannin came easing through the doors. He casually sauntered to the table where Isla was seated.

"The hell you got on your mind?" Kannin pulled out a seat and made himself comfortable. Isla hadn't even noticed him walk in.

She shook herself from her thoughts. "Reminiscing, that's all. How are you, handsome face?" She grinned.

Kannin shrugged his shoulders and ran his hands over his face. "I'm cool, sis. Stressed out a bit but shit iight."

Isla raised an eyebrow. "You is too young to be stressed out."

"I got grown man problems." He shot back.

"Hey, I gotta ask you something." Isla turned in her seat uncomfortably.

Kannin shot her a blank stare, waiting. "I'm listening."

"You might have been too young, but, uh, your brother used to hang with this older guy..."

"Dean." Kannin cut her off.

"Huh?" she asked, puzzled.

"Dean. His name is Dean. That's who you talkin bout." Kannin assured her. "What about him?"

Isla shook her head. "Oh, nothing. Was just asking."

Kannin stared at her for seconds, observing her demeanor, and he could sense she was lying, but he dropped it.

"Okay, so give me the update on school. What's new?" she questioned him, eager to hear.

Kannin laughed slightly, still shaking his head. "I ain't in school, Isla. I got bigger fish to fry. You know that."

"What?!" Isla raised her tone but quickly lowered her voice when she realized all eyes had been on her. "Kannin, what the fuck you mean?"

"I mean what I said," he sarcastically whispered back.

"You know what? You're coming to stay with me, and I'm enrolling you back in school," she demanded.

Kannin continued to shake his head. He leaned back in his seat and crossed his arms. "Isla, I am not a baby anymore."

Isla reached across the table and grabbed his hand. "Kannin, please. I'm sorry I left. But now I'm back. Let me fix this all." Her eyes began to water.

"Isla, none of this is your fault. I love your soul, my sister, but I do not need any handouts." Kannin spoke sincerely.

His phone chimed back-to-back mid conversation.

"I gotta go, sis," Kannin stated, looking in his phone. "I'll come through later on and stay with you for the night."

Isla nodded her head in approval. "That's fine with me. Be careful, bro. I love you."

"I love you, too!" He shouted before he hit the door.

Isla dropped her head and began to stuff her face. Helplessness took over. It was as if she was stuck in a spider web. While it was invisible, it had been strong. It was in the actions she couldn't take and the words she couldn't speak. She received several gut punches from her own fist.

Devyn sped down the street, eager to get to Isla. Rita mentioned to her that she gave Isla the job on the spot. Devyn felt accomplished, as if she knew Isla would be willing to reward her. She had pull indeed, but she wasn't aware she had that much pull.

Devyn arrived in no time and parallel parked on the street behind Isla. She took her sweet time creeping up the walkway to Isla's home.

I just know she goin put it on me, Devyn thought to herself with a grin plastered across her face.

She rushed the steps and entered unbeknownst. Isla checked her windows often and caught a glimpse of Devyn making her way, so she decided to head down and greet her.

"Caught me, huh?" Devyn shook her head and smirked.

Isla nodded. "I sure did." Devyn roamed her petite body and envisioned Isla ass naked without the robe. In fact, Devyn took it upon herself to snatch it from her body.

"Congratulations on the new job," she whispered before she began attacking Isla's neck with hundreds of kisses.

Isla didn't hesitate to spread her legs as Devyn's eyes feasted on her vaginal lips that were now puffed with arousal. Her pink pussy was smiling back at her, begging for her touch. Devyn placed one hand over her lips and, like a plier, opened them to see Isla's engorged clitoris come out of its sheath. The beautiful bundle of nerves it stored inside made her glisten.

Devyn stroked her firmly with two fingers as she spread her legs open even wider. Devyn instantly began to strum Isla like the strings on a guitar.

"Ouuu, don't stop," Isla groaned.

Devyn accelerated the strumming of her clit. She inserted two fingers inside Isla, who had now been releasing pent fluids. Devyn turned her hand inside her pussy, and like a cup, she curled her two fingers inside. She wanted to feel Isla's G-spot, the rubbery tissue that she wanted to extract her juices from. Devyn was determined to make her squirt. Once she located it, Devyn put pressure on the opposite leg to prevent them from closing. She moved her hand inside her vagina rapidly, back and forth, as if she were a vibrator.

"Fuckkkkk!" Isla wailed once more. She began to shake uncontrollably from Devyn stroking her. Her abdomen tightened. She could feel the grip on her hand. With one long, mighty scream, that went long and loud, Isla let out a torrent of squirt that gushed out of her charged pussy like a tap on full throttle. Her wetness smacked Devyn fully in the face, but it was so beautiful and warm and wet; she didn't mind.

Chapter 3

"Let's get this shit over with," Elon mumbled under his breath as he escorted Isla out. She followed closely behind him as they began to tour the facility.

"The purpose of the facility is to house perpetrators of crime." He sighed, rolling his eyes. "The most essential role is to ensure that prisoners can't escape."

Isla nodded, knowing that was common sense.

"And this is how we achieve that goal." Elon dramatically spun around slowly in a circle. Isla took it all in as she was surrounded by various barriers — large fences topped with rows of barbed wire, tall, brick walls, and several guard towers.

"Did they mean to design it like this?" Isla asked curiously.

Elon smirked. "Prison is designed to look imposing and threatening with no way of escape."

Isla nodded in approval and continued to follow behind him.

Beyond the boundaries of the security measures, Elon led her through the main gate, which she had familiarized herself with. "So, you already know this lil spot." He referred to the intake area. "This here is where inmates are checked in and assigned to a particular cell number. A large portion of the inmates' time is spent inside of their cell, which I'll show you shortly." He spoke and sauntered through the corridors with Isla on his heels.

"This is what we call a tier." Elon pointed through the gates. Cells were lined up side by side on the block where the general population of prisoners lived.

They continued to walk. "This is what the inside of a cell looks like." Isla examined the very sparse room and gasped for air.

"Unbelievable," she whispered.

It only consisted of a bunk bed, toilet, and little open space to move around.

"Down this hall," Elon continued, "this is what the staff refer to as their safe space in the workplace."

Elon extended his hand toward the room, and Isla was the least bit impressed. While the room created a large, inviting space, it still managed to be bleak. Lockers occupied the walls, and a variety of seating had been scattered throughout, nothing too fancy.

"Mmm, nice." Isla flashed a fake smile after her observation.

"Well, well, well..." Brooke tiptoed her way through the door, looking Isla up and down. She folded her arms. "Hello, newbie."

"Isla, this is Brooke, one of our head correctional officers." Elon made the introduction.

Isla rose her eyebrow in a surprised manner. *Oh, wow, that's nice. Wonder what you did to work your way up there,* she thought to herself. Flashing a fake smile, she waved.

Isla was highly attuned to energies, and she could feel Brooke's energy bleeding from her pores. She even carried a negative stench with her.

"Let's head to the library." He gently tapped Isla's arm.

Isla rolled her eyes and was on her way. Maneuvering through the corridors, Elon continued with his speech. "I'm going to assume you and Brooke have crossed paths." He snickered, lowering his head.

Isla nodded. "Yup, I know her from back in the day."

"I'll be honest. She's a handful so stay out her way," Elon stated.

Isla burst into laughter. "No, she better make sure she stay out my way. That's it; that's all."

Elon nodded and smirked, flashing his pearly veneers. "We

goin see." He allowed himself to examine her curves as she entered before him.

Isla instantly rose an eyebrow and let her bottom lip fall damn near to the floor. When Elon mentioned the library, she assumed a small, dark room in the bowels of the prison and a weary librarian toiling among old and outdated material. In her head, she pictured inmates creeping among the stacks and guards posted on alert, waiting for any signs of trouble. All in all, it had been the complete opposite. Isla disregarded the inmates for the moment and focused on the scenery at hand. The space had been bewitching with towering shelves, dim lighting, and the musty scent of books — aged and new. It seemed to transport her to a different time and place. Spanning every topic possible, it had been a scholar's paradise.

"Good morning, I'm Stacey Ann." The librarian extended her hand and welcomed Isla. "This is what the staff like to call my sanctuary." She joked, referring to the library.

"I'm Isla Harrison, the new psychiatrist." Stacey Anne grabbed her hand tightly and shook it firmly.

"It's so nice to have you onboard." Stacey Anne flashed a warm smile.

Elon's phone chimed, shaking him out of his trance. "Stacey, keep her occupied. I gotta take this call," he demanded.

Stacy Anne was average height with an extra bit of weight on her. She had a plump, round ass but small pennies for boobs. Her hair was cut into an asymmetrical bob, the color of platinum. A small gap between her two front teeth had been noticeable but didn't take away from the rest of her pearly whites that sat perfectly in her mouth. Her perfectly arched brows, fresh set of lashes, and manicured fingernails told Isla all she needed to know about her upkeep. But her soft butter pecan skin glowed and illuminated as she graced the room.

Inching farther inside, Stacey Anne broke the silence. "Ever worked in a prison before?"

Isla shook her head, nervously eyeballing the inmates who surprisingly had their focus in books.

Stacey Anne waved her hands in the air. "Oh, it's a piece of cake." She joked. "I will tell anyone that being a prison librarian is the hardest, most rewarding, saddest, happiest, challenging, eye-opening, and frustrating position around. They come with their fair share of challenges." She shrugged her shoulders. "But they also present opportunities not found anywhere else in this profession."

Isla was at a loss for words. Everything that she thought she knew about incarceration had gone out the window. She paused for a second and glanced at the inmates once more who happened to be in their own world.

"My hope is that I can aid in the rehabilitation process and, most importantly, provide a means of escape and distraction, so inmates stay out of trouble," Stacey Anne explained. "Idle hands are the devil's workshop in prison and having a book in them is much better than a weapon."

"I have so many questions," Isla mumbled. "Do you ever worry about your safety?" she asked.

Stacey Anne sucked her teeth. "Honey, in prison, there's a motto. Security is first. I'm sure you'll get your training on how to deal with dangerous situations and people."

Isla's eyes widened. "Huh? Training? Dangerous people?"

"You will be well taken care of." Stacey Anne assured. "The most draining aspect of my job was monitoring the inmates visiting the library while, at the same time, answering questions, performing legal research, and assisting patrons."

"Did you just call them patrons?" Isla asked out of curiosity.

Stacey Anne nodded. "I did. I always refer to the inmates as patrons when in the library. It makes the atmosphere professional, and I've been told multiple times how much I'm appreciated," she confessed. "But throughout my years here, I've learned to look two ways at one time and to be observant of my surroundings. Here and there, I would have to stop and zero in on a suspicious person. Sometimes, I've even had to raise my voice, and there have been instances I've dismissed the entire library due to horrible behavior."

Isla spun around slowly, taking a look at the inmates. "Okay, security is a first, and whether you're the librarian or not, you put security above all."

Stacey Anne nodded. "See, you catch on faster than most. I promise it's not that bad."

"I'm excited. I really am." Isla assured her.

"But you're also nervous. I can feel it." Stacey Anne challenged her. "You will do great, and besides, we need someone here to help these niggas get their mental on track." She joked, causing Isla to crack a smile. "For the most part, inmates who visit the library do so in order to get out of their cell and experience a change in scenery, like this one right here." She pointed to Gary, who was making his way to the door where they had been posted.

"Damn, Mrs. Stacey, who is dis?" Walking with a limp, he licked his lips, attempting to invade Isla's space, but Stacey Anne stepped in between.

"Boy, if you don't back your ass up. Don't come over here acting unruly. You know I do not play that shit," she sassed. Grabbing Isla's arms gently, they made their way to the center of the room as Stacey announced her presence. "Gentlemen, if I may, I'd like your attention." She cleared her throat. "This is Ms. Harrison, she's the new psychiatrist in the facility."

The inmates cooed and shouted; they blew kisses, and eyes were googly.

Isla was flattered but also nervous. Not only had she not been around a large group of men before, but to be in an enclosed space was different to her.

"Thank you all for the warm welcome. Like Mrs. Stacey mentioned, I am the new psychiatrist here. I look forward to meeting and getting to know you all as well." Isla stuttered through her sentence. "And you all don't have to call me Mrs. Harrison either. Just call me..."

"Isla." Kalei rose from the table where he had been seated in the far back near the corner, isolated. His now deep, baritone voice echoed throughout the room and sent chills down Isla's spine.

Kalei looked the same. While he had a bit more height on him, his skin was still rich and dark as before. His waves, that he ran his fingers across, sat on top of his head. Isla took note of his buff body build as he burst through his clothing. She couldn't wait to get her mouth on his lips. They stood in the same room, gazing at one another, as if no one else was in attendance.

Isla allowed her hands to fly to her chest as her breathing began to change. Time seemed to be slowing down, and she wasn't quite able to comprehend what she had been seeing. Like a form of mortal fear, she was unable to flee the situation. Instead, she absorbed it to its entirety.

Elon ended his call and turned on his heels. He cleared his throat. "I see you all met Ms. Harrison. She'll be attending the ceremony tomorrow. I need everyone on their Ps and Qs."

He gently grabbed Isla by her arm, leading her out the door. "We gotta cut this short. Let me show you your office." Isla nodded but quickly snapped her neck. She didn't want to let Kalei out of her sight.

On Elon's heels once again, she followed closely behind him through the corridors.

"Here we go." Coming to a halt down the wing, Elon swung the door open and allowed Isla to enter first.

"Ouu, okay." Isla took in the decor and scenery of the space. A dark walnut bookcase lined the entire lefthand wall. A leather sofa sat in the corner with a fur rug under it. It was accompanied with an Indian blanket draped over the arm. A corner desk with metal legs and a high back leather chair sat in the opposite corner. The far wall had a fireplace built in and a mantle dominating the center with shelves lining each side. On the mantle sat an antique clock with a painting of three jazz musicians. It was small but cozy and comfortable for her, very tidy and no clutter. Two small end tables and chairs occupied the center of the room for counseling.

"This all me?" Isla turned to Elon and titled her head, raising her eyebrow.

He smirked and nodded before he walked off. "Make yourself at home. I'll come check on you later." His voice disappeared down the hall as he did.

Once inside, she shut the door. Putting her back to the wall, she slowly slid down, sighing deeply.

"We found our way back to one another," she whispered to herself, teary eyed.

A loud thud shook her from her thoughts, causing her to jump up from the floor. She swung her office door open and was met by Devyn.

"I need a session, girl." Devyn joked with a seductive tone.

Isla flashed a fake smile. "Uh, now isn't a good time." She gently pushed Devyn back into the hall as she was trying to enter.

"Come on, boo. I just wanna taste it." Devyn insisted as she fondled her, gripping her tightly.

Isla shoved her backwards. "I said not right now!" She raised her tone, and Devyn could see her chest heaving up and down as she stumbled to catch her balance. Isla's skin began to turn red, and Devyn caught a tear running down her face.

"Babe, talk to me." Devyn tried once more to rush Isla, but she wasn't having it.

"Not right now, Devyn." She was firm with her response. Devyn finally got the picture and stepped off. She instantly reached for her phone as she headed down the hall and shot Isla a text. It was unusual to see her act in that manner.

Isla shut the door and fell back into the same position as before. She shook her head as thoughts of her past with Kalei invaded her mental.

There were three doors that lead to the small dirt path known as the yard — the main hallway door, the front hallway door, and the tower door. A few benches sat to the side, and there was a small gym area, an American flag, and some tables near the entrance across from the guard area. Inside the workout area sat two bench presses and treadmills. The bench presses weren't solid, but the treadmills worked perfectly fine.

The yard was the only outdoor area legally accessible to inmates. This was the only time inmates had the chance to interact with one another.

Kalei sat in the corner at the top of the bench. He scanned the yard, observing everything in sight.

Isla crossed his mind, and while he was focused, he couldn't seem to shake her presence here in the facility, but he pushed her to the back as he was in that mode. Kalei scanned the yard with a one-track mind, ignoring all distractions. He put on his game face and absorbed it all as he paid close attention.

Throughout the years, Kalei had learned the most effective way to win a battle was to avoid it by knowing what to look for ahead of time. Within his first month, he had learned to identify pre-fight indicators, using them to gauge his response before shit ever popped off.

The strange silence had him on high alert. Inmates began to gather in groups, while others appeared to be on the lookout.

Kalei stood slowly, making an exit. He calmly headed for the door. Still cautious of his surroundings, he kept his eyes open and head up.

"Oh, hell naw!" an inmate shouted as he watched Chico, a known junkie, overdose. The men stared at the scene in awe.

Chico began to foam at the mouth. The sudden stiffness in his arms and body caused him to hit the ground in almost an instant. Shaking uncontrollably, the whites of his eyes were now bloodshot red.

"Out the way!" Guards rushed the yard to assess the situation. Once the alarm had been sounded, everyone went back to their normal routine and headed back to their cells.

The fuck? Can't be, Kalei thought to himself. He shook his head and galloped to his cell.

Once alerted, Isla found herself in the east wing of the prison where the infirmary was located.

"Oh, you've got to be kidding." Isla frowned and instantly turned her nose up. The silence was eerie in the wing, littered with creepy medical devices that seemed as if they had been left behind from nearly centuries ago. The ghastly screams of injured inmates echoed throughout the halls which indicated something wasn't right. Isla glanced through the double windows; the macabre scene of inmates lying on their death beds made it clear that something terrible was in the works. The entire unit gave her a sinister feeling as if she were to be harmed. Morbid visions of the plague persisted as she toured the long, isolated wing.

Isla's heart throbbed as she saw firsthand how the prison environment would beat the empathy right out of you. The inmates and their illnesses were the least of the staffs' concern. Death from neglect was unheard of.

Isla's heels hit the cold, institutional, tile floor; she could be heard from a mile away. Coming to a halt, she gasped for air, grabbing her chest. She stopped at the door where Rita had been awaiting her arrival.

The small space had been dominated by a bed with a bedside table in the corner. Isla took note of how they attempted to create a restful vibe, but it came off as akin to a decorators' choice for a funeral home.

"Nice of you to join us." Rita rolled her eyes and folded her arms. "Send him to the hole after he comes to." She spoke directly to the nurse.

"The hole?" Isla questioned with a screwed face. "I've went to school with casual weed smokers and worked various jobs with weekend coke snorters, but I wasn't prepared for this," she confessed.

Rita chuckled slightly. "Well, you better get prepared. One, the addicts will continue the drug use, and two, the rest of us will pay for the mess they're making," she explained. "They're desperate with little to organize their days around besides the next fix. Getting high is their whole bid."

Isla nodded in approval. "I understand to a certain extent. But you're incarcerating people for addictions and then not giving them adequate treatment; that's a silent distrain." Isla expressed her concern. "This what they mean by being failed by the system."

Rita sighed deeply, maintaining her composure. "Get with the program, Harrison." She patted her shoulder before she walked off, leaving Isla in deep thought.

Prayer was one of the five pillars of Islam. Completing the five daily prayers in the way taught by Prophet Muhammad was an obligation for Kalei and was strictly required. He believed that communication with Allah was critical to strengthening his faith as a believer. He believed that Allah spoke to him through the Quran, and salah was his means of responding to Allah.

Five times each day, Kalei bowed down to Allah in a scheduled prayer. He conducted his prayers with heartfelt intentions, full attention, and devotion. He made sure his body was always clean after performing the correct ablutions, and he knew it was just as important to perform his prayers in a clean place.

While standing, he began. Raising his hands up in the air, he spoke. "Allahu Akbar." Folding his hands over his chest, he then recited the first chapter of the Quran in Arabic. Then, he recited other verses of the Quran that had been speaking to him. He raised his hands up again and called out, "Allahu Akbar." Bowing, he then recited three times, "Subhana rabbiyal adheem." He rose to a standing position and recited, "Sam I Allahu liman hamidah. Rabbana wa lakal hamd." He raised his hands up, calling out, "Allahu Akbar," once more. Prostrating himself on the ground, he recited three times, "Subhana Rabbiyal A'ala." Rising to a sitting position, he recited, "Allahu Akbar," prostrating himself again in the same manner before rising to a standing position, concluding the rak'ah. Then, he began again from the third step for the second rak'ah. After the completion of his two rak'ahs, he remained seated, reciting the first part of the Tashahhud in Arabic then the second part. Turning to his right, he said, "Assalamu alaikum wa rahmatullah." He then turned to his left and repeated the greeting, concluding his prayer. Now, it was time for the workout.

Kalei ignored the thick, grey, stone walls of his six by

four-foot cell. Instead, he diverted his focus to the mean barred opening with thick, metal bars and no glass. Kalei used his bed to perform his midday workouts, which happened to be a plank of wood on legs. The days varied. One day, the prison could be suffocatingly quiet, and other days, it could be pierced with screams of tortured inmates. But today, Kalei tuned it all out. Isla was the only thing on his mind, and he couldn't wait to get his hands on her.

He sighed loudly, slowing his pace as he was nearing his last set of fifteen reps. Speed hadn't been his focus. Instead, he wanted to feel the burn with a slow and controlled tempo.

"Fuckkkkk, Moe!" He managed to let out. He stood up, taking a minute to rest before he got back to it.

His mind was racing, and he couldn't seem to slow down his thoughts. With Isla in the picture, it was hard for him to think about anything else in that moment. As his anxiety increased, he began to feel uneasy. Instantly dropping to the floor, he started ten to fifteen reps for four sets of burpees. He knew, for one, that working out relieved his tension and stress, but somehow, he was still eager.

Brooke rounded the corridors in a hurry. She speed walked to Kalei's tier, which happened to be in the east wing. For the most part, she wanted to get the scoop on what he knew about Chino, but more importantly, she wanted some Vitamin D.

She snatched her keys from her waist and unlocked Kalei's cell, quickly slipping in. He ignored her presence and continued to work out. He counted to himself but mouthed the words.

Kalei had removed his shirt prior to his workout. Sweat trickled down his muscular frame. His dark chocolate skin glistened, sending chills down Brooke's spine. Focused, she watched him execute each exercise with precision, never once stopping to catch his breath. Brooke focused on his large rod swinging back and forth in shorts; her clit pulsated instantly. She wanted him. At that very moment, she wanted all of him.

Brooke's mouth watered. One flutter to her belly and she was done. Her heart rate increased, and she began to feel euphoric as she shut her eyes and replayed all the times Kalei had dicked her down in the past.

Her nipples, labia, and clitoris began to tingle. Brooke unbuckled her pants. Wasting no time, she allowed them to fall to her knees as she stepped out.

"Come tear this pussy up real quick, Daddy." She sauntered in his direction with a few steps, but Kalei didn't react.

Continuing his workout, he shook his head. "Nah, Brooke, go head. Not today."

"Nigga, what?" Brooke raised her tone. "I'm throwing all this ass at you, and you talkin bout some nah. Nigga, you ain't been sayin' that."

Kalei rose to his feet and invaded her space. He looked to the floor, bent down, and snatched her pants up on her waist roughly, causing her to stumble toward the door.

"I said not today. Get the fuck out, Brooke," he whispered

sinisterly through clenched teeth, shooting her a menacing glare.

Isla surfaced to his mind once more as he remembered his anxious attachment. He was relieved. In a sense, Isla made his troubles disappear.

Brooke said nothing. Instead, she took her time, straightened herself up, and found her way out. Brooke was Kalei's booty call, nothing more, nothing less. She had been taking care of his needs since he arrived, and today, all of that had changed. They had no emotional attachment whatsoever. She was only used for sexual encounters.

DRACO SLUGGISHLY MANEUVERED through the corridors. He spoke to a few inmates, who he had been cordial with, and dapped up a few acquaintances. But his mind was in another place, a place he was en route to. Draco hit the corner and wasted no time quickly sliding into the warden's office. He shut the door quietly and locked it behind him. Turning on his heels to face the warden, he grinned slyly.

"You already know what time it is." Draco clasped his hands, rubbing them together. He licked his lips.

Rita shook her head but couldn't help but blush, flashing a bright smile back at him. She rose from her seat and slowly undressed herself.

Draco picked Rita's tiny body up and dropped her on her

desk, planting electric kisses on her neck. His hands found her ass; Rita wrapped her arms around him, and the kisses intensified. He lifted her skirt and enjoyed the smell of her private area. Dropping to his knees, he started licking up her juices like a desperate man. Then, he slowly stuck his tongue inside her, running up her clit like a kitten. He gently flattened his tongue to touch her labia until he reached her clit. He continued sucking. Rita's moans were like music to his ears, knowing he was doing it just the way she liked. He rotated his hands and spread her legs farther, so he could have better access. In an instant, Rita began to fuck his face. Draco knew that was the signal for when she was about to explode, so he focused and sucked gently. He could feel her tensing up, and she arched her back, squeezing her eyes shut. Draco opened his mouth and allowed her to squirt across his face. Convulsing like never before, Draco let her relax for several seconds before spreading her legs once more. He kissed her entire body until their lips met. Rita reached for his hard cock and slowly led him inside of her.

Once inside, Draco savored how tight she was until he was all the way in. Pumping slowly, he continued to shower her with kisses, moving down to her breasts, taking each nipple into his mouth one at a time.

Draco threw Rita's legs over his shoulders, slowly going all the way inside and pulling out until the tip was at her entrance. They gazed into one another's eyes, not once blinking. Rita grinned seductively; Draco winked at her. He started to pump harder and faster, Rita tightened her muscles around his manhood, and they both trembled in unison. Draco let her legs drop from his shoulders, and still between her legs, he dropped another passionate kiss.

Neither ready to be done, Rita shoved him back then straddled him on top of her desk. She immediately began grinding back and forth. Draco loved it when she hopped on top; he never got enough of running his hands all over her body, making sure he gave her DD breasts extra attention. Now bouncing up and down, Rita bent forward, so Draco had both of her girls in his mouth. He ran his hands from her ass to her neck. Throwing her head back, he paid close attention and realized she was about to cum again. Draco could feel himself tightening up, and once he saw her face tense up, that was the cue.

"Ahhhhh!" They both let out a silent moan. Draco could feel her juices running down his rod. He pulled Rita into his chest, and they laid there as he started playing with her nipples. She reached down and slowly stroked his post ejaculated, sensitive cock, causing him to moan with her.

What started out as a couple of quick fucks and sucks turned into an everyday booty call. Draco had his eyes on Rita since he arrived. He constantly put himself into countless situations that required her assistance, just so he could get some time with her. Within a few short months, Rita had taken an interest in him. Though the relationship was built off of sex, the connection between the two grew strong. Draco developed feelings he never knew he had; Rita, on the other hand, didn't know how to feel. She cared for Draco, but she didn't know how to express the fact that she actually had feelings for an inmate — an individual who was years younger and a criminal. Not to mention, in the beginning, she started fucking him to make Elon upset, but now, she was all in.

ONCE ISLA MADE IT HOME, she dropped her clothes where she stood and headed to her bedroom. She laid in bed, awake, thinking of Kalei. She missed how they made love for the first time. She missed his soft lips kissing hers and his strong arms around her. She missed the sound of his raspy voice. She missed the feel of his hot breath on her neck while he slept beside her. She missed the feeling of his hands wandering around her naked body and the way he would smile at her while he explored. Isla shut her eyes and slid one hand between her legs, placing the other one on one of her breasts. She began rubbing her breast while she rubbed her clit slowly in a counterclockwise motion as she thought of Kalei eating her. Her wet tongue softly licked her lips before she bit her bottom lip, remembering how she used to suck his long, thick dick. She massaged her clit faster, pinching her nipple, thinking of Kalei's sweet mushroom top oozing his salty hot cum onto her tongue. She stopped and instantly shoved two fingers inside of her slick hole, thinking of how he used to bury his bone inside of her. She licked her middle and index finger as she pictured him fucking her slow in long strokes. She removed her fingers and continued rubbing on her swollen clit, imagining him pounding away. She rubbed her clit faster, thinking of how he used to look at her when he was close to reaching his climax. "Mmmmm, Kalei!" she shrieked out loud as she rubbed her clit as fast as she could. She thought of Kalei speeding up, moaning louder and louder as he made one final thrust into her. Her body began convulsing as she jerked repeatedly.

Chapter 4

While they were the best of friends, they were the complete opposite, but they balanced one another out. Kalei was laid back, quiet, and strategic, whereas Draco was a hot head and always in kill mode. He usually acted before he thought about the consequences. Kalei, on the other hand, always took the time out to weigh his options. When they were younger, Draco made sure nobody got out of line when it came to Kalei, and Kalei always made sure Draco stayed out of trouble; that was to the best of his ability.

Draco grew up terrorizing the streets for years. He was feared. Not because he was related to Dean, but because he created his own reputation. Dean's blood ran through his veins, no doubt; plus, he kept him under his wing. Draco caught his first body at the tender age of twelve. By the age of fifteen, he was robbing banks and drug dealers. Not to mention, he would kill anyone for some money, especially if it was owed to him. Draco was a firecracker, but he was smooth and bat shit crazy.

Kalei and Draco stood in the East Hall, taking turns pacing back and forth as they patiently awaited Dean's arrival.

"Fuck, Moe!" Draco whispered under his breath as he staggered back and forth.

Kalei shook his head. "We goin figure this shit out, bruh."

"Nah, why do I feel like somebody fuckin with us?" Draco thought out loud. "They doin it purposely."

Kalei stared into space as he pondered on the series of events. *This shit ain't no coincidence.*

Incarceration and overdoses were deeply entwined. As the crisis ravaged America, overdose deaths were sweeping through every corner of the nation, including behind the walls.

Dean eased around the corner of the corridor and graced Kalei and Draco with his presence.

"Talk to me, boys." He stood in place, clasping his hands together.

Both Kalei and Draco sighed heavily, running their hands down their faces.

"Man, that shit happened again." Draco went first.

"And it keeps happening, so it ain't no accident." Kalei added.

"Since when you start sellin bad dope, D?" Draco spread his feet apart. Changing his stance, he crossed his arms.

Dean smirked. "Nigga, I ain't never sold no bad shit. All my shit pure."

"Exactly!" Draco raised his voice as he got his point across. "That mean it's that bitch, Brooke!" He assumed.

Kalei shook his head but stayed silent as he carefully took Draco's assumptions into consideration.

"What would be her reason? And Brooke don't know shit about drugs," Dean argued.

Kalei shook his head. "Man, she got some good pussy, but I've known that bitch to be sneaky and conniving, so I ain't goin put it past her, D," he confessed.

Confusion plagued them all as halfcocked frowns spread across their faces.

It had been the eighth overdose in one week. A different body was dropping every day, and fingers were starting to be pointed. While Dean supplied the product, Kalei and Draco were in charge of distributing. So, all in all, the overdoses were on them.

Everyone had been wrapped up into their own thoughts, and Dean broke the silence. "Y'all niggas go get ready to walk," he demanded. "We'll figure this shit out. Better yet, I'll handle it. I've had enough of this shit."

Sighing, Draco dapped Dean up and went on his way; Kalei followed suit.

Kalei and Draco rushed to the courtyard, throwing their

gowns over their heads as they made their way. Once in attendance, Kalei stopped and scanned the crowd. Family and friends dressed in their Sunday's best awaited the soon-to-be college graduates. UDC joined the department of corrections to host a graduation ceremony for the inmates.

"You all have overcome many obstacles." Elon spoke out into the mic. He looked out at the graduation class. "Today is a very proud day for you and the people who are here today supporting you." The prison initiative was a four-year program that offered arts and education to prisoners. Once successfully completed, the inmates earned a bachelor's degree.

The graduating class, donning black gowns and caps with tassels dangling from atop, lined up outside a tent in the courtyard.

When Kalei put down his pen on his last exam, he was overjoyed. Never again would he have to stress over another exam. It was a release of pressure and a weight off of his shoulders. Excited was an understatement. The end to all of his hard work, the joy, the sweat, the tears, all resided in this moment. Incarceration had taken him across the states and allowed him to experience a wide range of environments. Kalei had witnessed everything from violent attacks on inmates and peace officers to a thousand guys of different ethnicities on a prison yard throwing up peace signs in a show of unity. But by far, his experience in the classroom helped him grow and shaped his life more than anything else.

Families stood, anxiously waiting, and they proceeded.

Smiles and waves soon filled the partially enclosed area as the sound of clapping echoed throughout. Loved ones blew kisses to those they recognized as they took their seats. As they waited for their names to be called, one by one, they walked, many waving to loved ones in the crowd and the administrators who handed out their hard-earned degrees.

"We have been given an incredible privilege with this education." A fairly popular inmate got up and spoke. "Now it's our turn to spread that knowledge." He turned his tassel and threw his cap in the air, causing the other to do the same; they rejoiced. They shared high fives and fist bumps with one another while looking over their newest achievement: a college degree.

Isla stood in the crowd like a proud parent. She felt like she was going to explode with pride. As she was extremely happy, she forgot about all the troubles in the world watching Kalei receive his diploma.

"Damn, bruh! Who would have ever thought?" Draco shouted jokingly.

Kalei shrugged his shoulders. "Nigga, we did it!"

Draco shook his head with a huge grin plastered across his face. "They told us we wouldn't be shit when they kicked us out of school."

"Now look at us, all degreed up, my boy!" Kalei reminded him.

Elon emersed from the crowd, ready to give another small speech. "This is the beginning of a new chapter in your personal stories," he began. "By giving, you've enriched the lives of others. Graduates, you have each excelled in so many ways through your gifts." The audience rose and gave a standing ovation. The inmates' faces showed joy and accomplishment through the ceremony.

Kalei scanned the room once more; he took note of Dean maneuvering through the crowds of people. As he passed Isla, Kalei caught her eye.

Isla always used to joke with Kalei about their eyes being the windows to one another's souls, but in actuality, they were the windows to their hearts. Isla and Kalei's eyes met as they stared at each other intensely. Their pupils increased, and Isla's glistening eyes told Kalei everything he needed to know and vice versa.

After the ceremony, Dean made his way to the administrative wing and found an empty office. Dean didn't have an office; he utilized whichever ones were in his reach at that moment. This office space, specifically the wallpaper, had been peeling, and the ceiling tiles were stained with water damage. The office only contained the essentials — a desk, a chair, and a lone lamp, devoid of any decorations or comforts.

Brooke didn't bother knocking; she entered without approval. Dean smirked and shook his head as he watched Brooke storm in the room somewhat seductively. "Good day, Brooke. I hope you been keeping an eye on that nigga, Ty, for me." He was straight forward and to the point.

Dean had eyes and ears everywhere in the streets, so he

wasn't surprised to hear that Brooke had her eyes on Ty. While the dick was immaculate, she had no idea he was a rat. Dean took it upon himself to exploit both Ty and Brooke; Ty was gullible, and Brooke was simply hot and horny. Not to mention, he pillow talked like a bitch, and he wasn't one to turn down pussy, so putting Brooke in his face was a piece of cake. She was money hungry and easy to manipulate. All Dean had to do was flash a couple of racks, and she was doing whatever for the coin.

Her assignment was to simply keep tabs on Ty and report his every move back to Dean. He wanted to know when he ate, when he slept, when he took a shit, and more.

She began tugging on her uniform. "I can do better than that. How bout I take care of you?" She twirled in a circle as she unbuttoned her blouse, allowing it to fall from her shoulders.

"Put your clothes back on please. I'm here for business, not pleasure," he demanded with a straight face.

Dean had not only known Brooke, but he had heard about her more than he liked to. If she wasn't fucking one of his men on the outside, she dang sure was giving it up behind the walls. The last thing he wanted to do was stick his dick inside her. "Now, again, have you been keeping an eye on that nigga, Ty, for me?"

She nodded while trying to redress herself. "Yeah."

There simply was no relationship with Dean and Brooke. Business was simply business with them, nothing more, nothing less. What she did was her business as long as it didn't affect his business; he made that clear from day one. Dean put Brooke on his payroll shortly after she was hired; the money was too good for her to resist. She did his dirty work, and he reaped the benefits, but on the bright side, when it came down to it, he wouldn't hesitate to defend her.

Dean knew she was doing whatever it took to be at the top, which was a plus. While it was complicated here and there getting the contraband into the prison, she did it and succeeded.

Dean nodded his head; silence filled the room for several seconds before he broke it again. "Can you tell me about them ODs?" Dean looked her in her eyes, studying her movements but also listening to the tone in her voice when she responded. He was itching to catch her in a lie. He knew for a fact he wouldn't hesitate to end her, but he prayed he didn't have to.

Brooke shrugged her shoulders, shaking her head from left to right. "No, sir."

Dean smirked. "Really? Why do some feel that you're the one who's been fuckin with my product?"

"What?!" she shouted. "Me? Why would I do that? I'm the one taking all the risk bringing the shit in." She defended herself. But Dean took note of her defensive reaction.

"I'm just going to say this. Don't let me find out it's been you this whole time. I promise you won't live to see the light of another day if I do." He threatened her and dismissed himself.

ISLA LEANED over her desk and skimmed through the inmates' files that she would be seeing on a daily. Running her fingers over the list, she came across Draco's name then Kalei's. Her heart fluttered and skipped a few beats instantly.

A hard knock at her office door shook her from her trance. Isla popped up, ready to greet her first client of the day. The correctional officer opened the door and allowed the inmate to enter. To her surprise, it was an old friend. Isla's eyes lit up.

"Long time no see!" Draco greet her as the guard uncuffed him and went on his way.

Isla pulled Draco in for a friendly hug and examined him.

"Yes, long time no see," she added. Excited, she didn't know where to start. "Okay, sit so we can get started."

Taking her seat, Isla finally grabbed Draco's folder and skimmed through it. She raised her eyebrow a few times, but she wasn't the judgmental type. She had known Draco her entire childhood, so reading half of the things listed in his profile was hard for her.

Draco was taller than he was the last time she laid eyes on him. He was more toned as well, thanks to the daily work-outs. His eyebrows connected to each other in the center, and he shot glares with his chinky, round eyes. His pale skin had been covered in graffiti from head to toe, inked up. He walked with a slight limp and picked at his chin hairs in the process.

"Draco, why do they make you seem like such a menace?" she whispered.

Draco grinned and shrugged his shoulders. "Isla, man, you know me. You know my heart, but you also know I don't tolerate no shit," he expressed.

Isla nodded and shook her head as she continued to skim through his files in silence. They had named Draco the most ruthless at a young age. Murder, robbery, drug dealing, and extortion were said to be his business, and he took them dead serious.

Isla leaned back and made herself comfortable. She continued to survey the files as she held them in front of her face with her pen to her mouth. "Murderer, that's what they call you," she whispered, continuing to nibble on the end of the pen.

Draco smirked and shook his head. "And."

Isla knew firsthand that there were different reasons for certain crimes, and the act may be spontaneous or even premeditated. "What drives you to kill? What do you serve by taking a life?"

Draco smirked once again, but he took a few seconds to ponder on his response. "You can look at a crime in many different ways. A murderer is a murderer, but all of us have different motives and some have no motive, other than an urge without any fear of the law and devoid of empathy."

Isla flashed a warm smile at his response as she wasn't expecting it. "That wasn't my question. Cold-blooded killings to assuage some urge. What was the urge? Was it your need to control, the desire for power, the thrill, was it pleasure? Are you remorseful; is there guilt? Is there empathy? Is there no conscience, Draco?" Isla bombarded him with questions.

Draco shrugged his shoulders. "It all depends on who you kill and why. I been in and out of institutions since a child, Isla. After a while, this shit don't feel like nothing. By the age of nine, I had lost everything, so for real, if we being honest, life to me didn't have much value." He paused to think for a second then began again. "Like I said, it's different for each person. It also depends on their personality, history, and immediate circumstances."

"Oh, yeah? How do you figure?" Isla challenged him.

"It's going to be different for a psychopath, an enraged lover, a woman who has been beaten and has just discovered her child has been sexually abused, the young man who carries a knife expecting to use it, the man who hunts his victims because he somehow conflates sexual excitement with the thrill of kill, a teenager who is tormented by voices." He paused to take a breath. "Guilt, anger, sickness, relief, disappointment, emptiness, it's a category of crimes that encompass a huge breadth of human experience. Consequently, you can't pin it down to one thing and one feeling," he explained.

Isla set his files in her lap. She crossed her arms and gazed into Draco's eyes. His responses had been detailed and came unexpectedly. Draco's decisions were based upon emotion and reason, and some days, he favored one over the other.

Emotionally charged situations allowed him to act impulsively, ignoring rationality.

"Okay, let's go back to what you said, you being in and out since a kid. How has prison changed you?" Isla asked.

Draco sighed and fell back into his seat. He shrugged his shoulders. "Day after day, year after year, imagine having no space to call your own, no choice over who to be with, what to eat, or where to go. Threat and suspicion are everywhere, love or even a gentle touch can be difficult to find, you're separated from family and friends." He paused, shrugging his shoulders again. The institutions had altered his spatial, temporal, and bodily dimensions, weakening his emotional life and undermining his identity.

Draco leaned forward in his seat; he clasped his hands together. "You not allowed to be weak in here. There's a level of respect towards others. Blowing your nose at the dinner table can get you killed in here. You can't run and hide from your problems in here; therefore, you're forced to face them. PTSD is unavoidable." He rambled and sighed loudly before he continued. Isla just sat there and listened. She let him have the floor.

"It ain't been all bad though," he confessed. "It's taught me humility and how to appreciate the simple things life has to offer. It's taught me to take nothing for granted. It changed the way I look at life and how I look at myself. Now don't get me wrong. The change was a slow process, but to be honest, Isla, this shit challenged me to be better and do better, in and out of prison, even though I know I ain't gettin out," he expressed.

Isla continued to gaze; she nodded her head in amazement. As evil and dumb as they had painted Draco out to be, he was the complete opposite. While he committed crimes, he still knew right from wrong, along with the consequences that stemmed from his actions.

"Okay, so now tell me this." Isla turned uncomfortably in her chair, leaning forward in the same position as Draco. "Your line of work, why'd you choose it? The drugs? That lifestyle in particular?" She pried.

Draco chuckled and threw his hands in the air. "My line of work is thrilling, Isla." He half joked with a smile plastered on his face, which caused her to crack a smile. "Naw, for real though, a motherfucker who looking for excitement and who want an expensive lifestyle, they often resort to drug dealing, not just because of the money, but they might even be bored." He shrugged his shoulders. "That's why you can find even the most well-educated peoples with good jobs dealing." Isla's eyes widened, and Draco shook his head. "Yeah, I said it. That shit creates the life people want. It's that simple."

"So, what about you? What was your reasoning?"

Draco sighed and grinned. He swung his leg across the other. "Three main reasons." He threw up three fingers. "Money, money, and money. It's simply a better paying position… for the people that see it that way of course."

"What about the risks though? Does that ever surface in your mind?" she interjected.

He nodded slowly. "For sure. Some see the risk and decided it don't pay enough but not I." He assured. "Supply and demand. You identify the need in your community and find a way to fill it. If you got something that the people want and a means to get it to them, you goin make you some money. It's just good business, Isla," he explained. "Duhhh!" He blurted out. The two erupted into laughter. Draco would shout that out often when they were younger. It automatically brought back memories.

"Oh, my God, you still do that shit?" Isla mumbled as they laughed in unison.

"Man, look. I enjoyed this time to talk to you. Ion really be talking to folks besides bruh, and shit, we don't really be on shit like this," Draco expressed.

"I'm always here if you need to talk about anything, Draco. Friends for life, remember?" Isla grabbed his hand and squeezed it, showing her sincerity.

"Say less. I appreciate you, sis." Draco stood and pulled her in for a tight hug before he prepared to made his exit.

While she had known him since a child, she still didn't really know him. His parents weren't around, he had no siblings, no guidance, nothing. Why he acted out hadn't been the mystery. Isla wanted to get to the root of the cause.

The soft knock on the door indicated that their time was now up. Isla sighed and flashed a fake smile. She was enjoying their discussion and didn't want it to end. Once Draco was cuffed and out the door, the sight of Kalei entering her office made her heart skip a beat. The guard shut the door and was out of sight, leaving an awkward silence lingering in the air. Their eyes met instantly as they stood on opposite sides of the room, a great distance away from one another.

Kalei stood in front of her, causing her entire body to become tight and rigid; she was stiff as was he. Kalei's chest tightened while Isla's breathing became shallow before she lunged into his arms.

"Okay, so, what happened that night?" Isla broke the silence.

Kalei sighed, swaying left to right, holding her still in his arms. "Snatched me up, conspiracy to distribute cocaine and some more shit," he explained.

"Fuckin with Dean," Isla whispered under her breath, shaking her head.

"Man, fuck that. We need to handle some things," Kalei demanded.

Kalei stopped in his tracks as his eyes drank her in. His face broke into a devilish half smile, and he inched closer toward her. Kalei gently placed kisses on Isla's lips and stared into her eyes. Slowly but not wasting any time, they undressed one another. His cock bobbed as he flexed. Isla reached for him with her free hand. He was so warm and hard as he lurched under her touch. She allowed her fingers to explore his cock as his breathing became sharper. His shaft was long and thick, and she could feel his veins bulging at the sides. Running her thumb over his tip, she soon had it slick with his pre cum. Isla dragged her manicured nails down the sensitive underside of his cock, making him groan before she cupped his balls. Having enough of the teasing, Kalei roughly scooped her up in his arms. He placed her on top of her desk and spread her legs instantly. He took his manhood and rubbed himself all over her clitoris. Isla moaned in delight. Kalei pushed his way inside her slowly. He paused when he entered, and they gazed into each other's eyes. Without blinking, they held that stare. Isla squeezed her muscles around him. Their breathing became tense through their nostrils. Thrusting at a fast pace, Isla moaned softly. She took her free hand and began to circle her clit with two fingers and felt a deep stirring in her body. The vibration seemed to billow from within and radiated through her entire body. Reveling in the large, thick cock deep inside her, Isla knew she would soon be cumming. The tension built within her as she knowingly mashed her wet fingers into her clitoris. It felt as if the world was about to explode into a billion glorious pieces as the power of her orgasm took over.

Devyn sauntered down the halls and crept around the corridors of the east wing. She scanned the halls with only one thing in mind — getting to Isla. Inching closer toward the door, the stench of wet pussy being pounded filled the air; she knew the smell from anywhere. The sound of Isla's moans could be heard as Devyn pressed her ear against the door.

Her chest started to burn, and she became lightheaded. All in all, she didn't know how to feel, and confusion plagued her. For years, she had never seen Isla with a man, so this was new to her. Hurt and anger consumed her. She had given Isla an opportunity and here she was, ruining it. Devyn backed away from the door and made a mental note of the encounter. She decided to confront Isla at her home when her shift ended.

This bitch got some explaining to do, she thought to herself, turning on her heels away from Isla's office.

Isla paced around her fair-sized office space. She buttoned her top and redressed herself. Kalei did the same. He eyeballed Isla, admiring her curves that she had grown into and more.

"Let's talk, babe." Isla began. "You go first."

Kalei smirked as he continued to dress himself. "I come home in some days. I think ten or less," he confessed.

Isla snapped her neck in his direction, not knowing how to feel inside. "Kalei, are you serious, or are you fuckin with my head?"

"I'm serious, boo." He grinned, falling back into the loveseat that occupied her corner. "But let's talk. I been needing someone to talk to, and plus, I miss you, girl."

Isla shook her head and took her seat. Crossing her legs, she slid his files from her desk and skimmed through them.

"So, why'd you do it?" she questioned him, not once giving him any eye contact, still focused on the documents.

Kalei rolled his eyes and sighed. "You know the answer, Isla."

"I don't," she sassed. "So, let me hear it."

Kalei sighed loudly once more. "The attainment of an income that is very much unattainable for people like us coming up in the type of neighborhood we from. The shit just made sense to me, Isla," he explained. "Back then, yeah, it made me feel older, more capable, trustworthy, and responsible; there's a list of shit."

"Well, what about the risk?" she asked, raising her eyebrow in confusion.

"Even with the risks, that shit solves a problem, and on top of that, it earned you respect." He chuckled. "Shit, even in here, this shit became a rite of passage."

Isla fell back into her seat and gazed into Kalei's eyes, taking in all his features, remembering who she had known years prior. While his looks had differed slightly, he, as a person, hadn't.

Back in the day, Kalei and Draco were public enemies, distributing sixty percent of the cocaine that flooded the streets. When Draco got booked, Kalei took it on alone. At his peak, he was selling two thousand kilos a week while reaping the gross profits of seventy million a month. Dean ran the operation with over one hundred and fifty men supporting him, Kalei being at the top of his list.

"Dean." She stared blankly as she was never too fond of him.

Kalei laughed, shaking his head. "What about him?"

"Where did you even find him?" she sassed.

"Mannnn." Kalei sucked his teeth and waved her off. "Statistically, I'm supposed to be dead, in jail, or homeless."

"Your point?" Isla rolled her eyes.

"How didn't I end up another statistic? One caring adult," he explained. "Dean found me. He consistently and intentionally invested time in me, making a positive and significant difference in my life."

Isla's expression softened, and she put herself in Kalei's shoes for once.

"We ain't have parents, Isla. Remember that. Moe wasn't shit, so Dean the closest thing I got to a father figure. I'm grateful as hell for that man. Love his soul," he expressed with teary eyes.

A knock on the door startled them both, causing them to jump slightly. "Times up, inmate." The guard entered without notice.

"Damn, that was short as hell." Kalei balled his face up.

"You and I both know why." Isla smirked, whispering under her breath. "I'll see you tomorrow, sir." She put on a facade for the guard that had been doing the escorting. Kalei turned his back to the officer. Walking backwards, he winked then blew a kiss in Isla's direction, causing her to blush hard.

After the recent events, her mind was spiraling. She paced a small space in the room, back and forth. "What the fuck is really wrong with you, dude!?" Brooke raised her voice.

Changing her tone, she challenged Elon. "All these fuckin overdoses and it's been your ass this whole time!"

"I need you to calm the fuck down and lower your tone," he demanded sternly. "Now, if you'd relax, you will know I have it all worked out. Nobody will ever know you had anything to do with it."

Brooke scoffed. "Nigga, is you serious right now? I ain't have nothing to do with it at all. All I did was bring it in and put it in your hands."

"And now you're guilty by association." He laughed hysterically.

Brooke rolled her eyes and threw her hands on her hips. "What's really your motive? What exactly is your angle?"

"Mind the business that pays you," he informed her.

Elon was doing whatever it took to see Dean crumble. That was what he wanted, to see his baby brother hit rock bottom. As Dean was keeping the prison stocked up with the best of best drugs, Elon was doing his part and making sure the overdoses skyrocketed. His goal was to make Dean look bad; he despised the way people admired him and glorified him.

"Do you even know who you fuckin with? I wouldn't even dare. Yeah, Kalei and Draco the main men, but them drugs belong to Dean," she expressed.

Elon sucked his teeth. "Bitch, you think I don't know that? Fuck Dean and his little workers! As soon as I get the chance, them motherfuckers goin straight to solitary, and I ain't lettin' them out," he confessed.

Brooke smirked, folding her arms. "E, do you even have the authority to do that?"

Keeping his cool, he ran his hands through his goatee. "Listen here, Brooke, I have a lot more authority than you think I do. How bout you try your hand and see if you have a job tomorrow morning?" He flashed his pearly white teeth before he backed out of the door, leaving Brook standing there.

KANNIN CAUGHT an Uber to Isla's spot after he finished his business. He was following in his brother's footsteps, trappin' day and night. Business was booming, and he was determined to make his trap thump. He wasn't letting anybody get in his way either, and that was a fact. Since Kalei had gotten booked, the streets were dubbin Kannin as the younger but more ruthless of the two. Money was his motive; he refused to go back poor. Moe had made their childhood a living hell for her foster children, and now that he was older, he promised to never look back.

Having Isla back in town was somewhat a relief for him. Though he was damn near already on his own, having her in his corner was a plus. He trusted her with his life, and he knew she would go to war for him if need be. They had been bonded since children. She was the older sister he never had. She protected him by any means, and that never changed. The love he had for Isla was out of this world.

SZA's *Snooze* shook him from his thoughts as the tunes rang out. Isla was cruising down the street with the hit blasting. Kannin shook his head and laughed as he watched Isla's head move from left to right while she lip sync.

"Same ole Isla," he whispered to himself as he stood.

"Ahhhh, you made it!" Isla shouted as she emerged from the car after putting it in park. "My heart is so full with joy!" She carried on dramatically as she retrieved her belongings. Kannin approached to help, grabbing bags.

"Damn, the fuck you got in here?" He half joked as he had a bit of trouble carrying one bag.

"Oh, please, you got it." Isla waved him off as she walked in front of him.

She skipped up the three porch steps. Shoving her key in, they entered within seconds.

Kannin's mouth dropped at the sight of Isla's renovated, new home in southwest. "Damn, sis, I ain't know you was doin it like this."

Kannin looked around and took in the exquisite interior design of Isla's new home. The lighting, the furnishings, the art on the wall, the newly renovated appliances, he marveled at it all.

"I told you to come live with me," she sassed. "When

Kalei come home, we moving though. We might need something bigger."

Kannin rose his eyebrow. "He coming home soon."

"Oh, I know." She blushed. Finding the remote, she flipped through the channels. "We had a long talk today."

Kannin shook his head and fell onto her sofa. "Oh, hell naw! I know what that look means!" He covered his face with a pillow to muffle his screams. Isla burst into laughter. "You went to see him?" Kannin questioned. "I go for my visit in a couple days."

Isla nodded her head, still blushing. "I get to see him whenever I want." She smirked. "I got a position at the facility."

"Damn, you lucky! Get to see that nigga all the time." Kannin spoke with a hint of jealousy in his voice.

"He will be home very soon." Isla assured once more.

Kannin snatched the remote from Isla's hand quickly. He flipped through the channels as if he didn't just take the remote from her. Stuck, she sat there in amazement.

"Yeah, we bout to watch *The Wire*," he stated, nodding his head in approval.

Isla laughed hysterically; Kannin stared at her in confusion. "Nigga, what your young ass know about *The Wire*? That shit came out before you were even born! Let alone thought of!"

Kannin smirked and shrugged his shoulders. "I know a lil something."

The two laughed and cracked jokes for the remainder of the night. Isla filled him in on her college journey, and he filled her in on life growing up with Moe. Isla listened and let him vent; Kannin expressed his deepest, darkest secrets, and Isla allowed him to be vulnerable with her. She coddled him as if he were a small boy again. Eight episodes in, they were both pissy drunk, making their way up to Isla's room.

Kannin watched Isla sleep peacefully in a drunken slumber. He was rewarded with the relaxed look on her face and her perfectly shaped breasts staring up at him. He took in all of Isla's beauty as he explored her body. He slid in closer to her and began to caress her entire body. Starting with her legs, he gently massaged her calves and thighs. He moved higher as his hands traced her stomach in circles around her belly button.

"Kalei..." Isla whispered under her breath. She was enjoying Kannin's touches and caresses as she thought he was Kalei.

Inching closer, not in her right mind, chills went through her body. Their eyes met in an instant. Kannin grabbed behind her and kissed her passionately. He allowed his hands to work their way down from her chest to her panties. Kannin slid his finger past her clit and was surprised at how wet she had already been. Taking his time, he planted kisses all over Isla's body. She moaned and groaned as she envisioned Kalei dominating her. Kannin gently began tracing his tongue over her breast. Starting at the outer most edges and working inward toward her hardening nipples, he took each nipple into his mouth separately. Rolling it around with his tongue, he gently sucked, bringing it to its max hardness then nibbling slightly.

Heavily intoxicated still, Kannin took his time settling in a comfortable position. Starting with her feet, he kissed and traced his tongue up her legs, reaching her inner thighs. He marveled at the fact that he was in between her legs at the moment. He slowly grabbed her panties and pulled them down. Leaning backwards, he admired her pussy, every inch of it. He moved in and carefully licked the entire length of her outer lips, sucking and nibbling away. He wanted to dive right in, but he knew it'd be much more pleasurable if he continued to take his sweet time. After he thoroughly wet her outer lips, his tongue went in full length like a spear. Dipping in and out, running his tongue up and down, Isla's body was beginning to respond. Her hips were undulating upward to meet his tongue's advances. He allowed his tongue to fully penetrate as she released long moans. Kannin took his time devouring her clit. Taking each lip separately into his mouth, he sucked gently but hard, stripping them of any juices. He inserted his fingers into her drenched pussy, taking Isla's breath away. She clamped down on his fingers as he continued to flick his tongue over her sensitive clit. Her hips took over, and she began fucking his fingers. Her legs slowly began to clench, and Kannin knew what that meant. He loved every minute of it. It turned him on to have his head clamped down in between her legs. Isla's body jerked violently as Kannin continued his routine.

"Ohhhh, my God." Isla panted with her eyes shut tight. Groggy, she squirmed.

Kannin swung Isla's body over and sat her on top of him. She leaned from side to side until she caught her balance using his chest; she straddled him.

"Kalei..." she mumbled again.

Kannin's mind went crazy knowing what was coming. This was a special treat for him. Isla lowered her body down onto his as she reached down and took his rod into her hands. She rubbed his head slowly over her drenched clit. Kannin's hands crept up her body, and she lowered herself more, so he could take them each in his mouth. She could feel his manhood jerk as his mouth came in contact with her breast. She rose up slightly, watching as he expressed disappointment. That quickly disappeared as he felt the tip of his penis dive into her wetness. Isla slowly eased her body down onto Kannin's cock. She could feel him jerk and throb inside of her as her muscles adjusted to his size. Kannin almost passed out as a mini orgasm ripped through his body. She rocked her hips back and forth, and his hands rested on her ass. Isla moaned as Kannin massaged her nipples while she was now bouncing up and down. Isla fell into his chest, and Kannin took over. He grabbed both of her cheeks firmly. Arching his back, he brought his hips from the bed and began a rapid fucking motion. The sound of their bodies slapping together filled the room. Isla broke out into an orgasm. Kannin could feel her juices escaping, running down his thighs. He kicked into overdrive, pounding away for all that was worth it. He felt his cum boiling up and passing through his shaft. Just like that, he shot his thick cum deep inside Isla's body. Their moans filled the room. Both gave out from the intense orgasm and the alcohol. Isla rolled to the opposite side of the bed and passed out. Kannin lie there with his rod still rock hard, ready and wanting more, until he drifted off to sleep.

After the series of events that took place today, Devyn was still furious. With a sinister mug plastered on her face, she drove through the streets. Her hands shook and cheeks were burning from anger. She began to shake as she clenched her jaw. Squinting her eyes, she curled her lips. Devyn didn't understand what unrequited love was at the time, but she was finding out in the process. While they occasionally shared a deep level of intimacy, Isla did not reciprocate the mutual feelings.

She parallel parked on Isla's street. Hopping out, she rushed the front door. Instead of causing a scene, she played it smart and used her spare key Isla gifted her with. Devyn crept inside, quietly shutting the door behind her.

She inched her way deeper into the home. The volume on the television had been at its max, louder than usual, and the lights were still on. Devyn examined the living room and noticed another set of items - men's items.

No the fuck, this bitch didn't, she thought to herself as she rummaged through the belongings. She turned on her heels with a menacing glare and headed for the stairs. Devyn tiptoed up each step until she reached Isla's master bedroom.

She gently pushed the door open slowly and gasped for air.

Isla was sprawled onto the bed ass naked, as was Kannin, who laid right next to her. They were both stretched out in a drunken slumber, and Devyn could smell the alcohol leaking from their pores. She stood frozen in amazement as she stared at Isla.

"Isla!" Devyn shouted. "Get the fuck up! And who the fuck is this nigga?"

Both Isla and Kannin jumped from their sleep. They stumbled off the bed, snatching the sheets to cover their naked bodies and give distance between them and Devyn. Always on point, Kannin retrieved his .39 revolver that he managed to carry with him. He had her tucked under the pillow just in case.

"I'll blow this bitch head clean off her shoulders right fuckin now, Isla," Kannin stated with clenched jaws. "Fuck is this bitch?" he asked, looking Devyn up and down.

Confused and discombobulated, Isla knew she would have time to figure out why she was naked in bed with Kannin, but at the moment, she stood between the two and attempted to alleviate the situation.

"Put the gun down," Isla whispered, making eye contact with Kannin. She moved slowly and made sure all her moves were calculated. The last thing she wanted to do was get her head blown off by him. Once he lowered the weapon, she focused her attention back to Devyn.

"Who the fuck do you think you are, coming in my shit like this?" Isla shouted with frustration. She wrapped the thin sheet tighter around her body as it continued to slide down. "Middle of the night and you starting shit! This ain't that, Devyn." She clarified. "Real shit, I don't know wassup with you," she sassed.

Devyn smirked. "Bitch, is you serious? Since when did you start liking niggas? First, I catch you red handed fuckin an inmate. Now this?" She pointed in Kannin's direction. "Not to mention, I got you that job! I put you on!" She beat on her chest. "Then, I come in here and you laid up wit a nigga."

Isla turned red. She had no idea Devyn overheard her and Kalei.

Kannin stood in the corner, unfazed, as he watched Isla and Devyn both plead their cases. He shook his head and smirked. "She pushing it."

"Nigga, fuck you and mind your business!" Devyn shot back. "Fuck you even doing here?"

Kannin laughed hysterically, purposely antagonizing her. "Isla is my business. She also the only reason your head is still attached to your shoulders." He reminded Devyn. "And since you are skating on thin ice, I think it's time for you to get goin, homegirl," he recommended.

Devyn looked back to Isla for support, but she said nothing.

"That's it? We done?" Devyn asked in a low tone as her voice cracked. She did her best holding back tears. "Like none of this was ever anything to you?" She sucked her teeth and made an exit.

Isla sighed loudly, running behind Devyn. "We've been the best of friends for years, D," she shouted down the hall. "You just wanted it to be more than what it was." Isla managed to get out, but Devyn had already hit the door and slammed it shut on the way out. She rushed down the steps to lock the door behind her, and she scooped up her spare key in the process; Devyn left it behind purposely.

Isla's head was spinning, and she still couldn't pinpoint how she ended up ass naked in the bed with Kannin. Her mind had gone completely blank after guzzling back-to-back shots of tequila. *Oh, my God, what if Kalei finds out?* she thought to herself, and she made her way back upstairs.

"You fuckin bitches, sis?" Kannin joked with her. "I would have killed that bitch. You know that?"

Isla shook her head and sighed loudly. "Devyn and I were friends. We went to school together; she had a thing for me, but I told her way back that I didn't get down like that, ya know?" Isla pulled the thin sheet around her body once more and took a seat at the edge of her bed. "She always wanted it to be more. I was, and still am, super grateful for my position at the facility, but now I feel like she's going to fuck that up." Isla thought back to her sexual encounter with Kalei earlier in her office.

"Of course, she caught you and my brother." He smirked. "But you let that bitch lick your pussy, didn't you?" He laughed but turned his nose up.

Isla shook her head, trying to hold back her grin. "Hell yeah, she did, more than a few times." They both burst into laughter.

Isla went with the flow and tried to make light of the situation, but deep inside, she was still confused.

"Kannin, did we fuck?" Isla broke the awkward silence. "Yes or no?"

Kannin sat in silence, then he nodded his head. He didn't have a response. He didn't know how to apologize either. He knew he was in the wrong, and nothing should have gone down between them.

"Fuckkkkkkk!" Isla shouted.

Devyn stood in Ty's foyer, pacing back and forth.

There was nothing left of her happiness. Everything was gone. She could hardly keep herself together. She began to shake. Her lower lip quivered, and her eyes seemed to lose their sparkle as tears started to roll down her cheeks.

"Bitch had the nerve to be fuckin one of the inmates," she expressed. "And I got the bitch the job!"

Ty laughed silently, shaking his head. "These bitches vicious, man. Look at how she repaid you." He chimed in.

Ty rolled his blunt as he listened to Devyn vent and pour her heart out. Ty and Devyn were first cousins, which made them one another's first friend. Both grew up on the outskirts of the city; Ty just portrayed himself to be someone he was not. Growing up, the two were inseparable, and Ty always looked out for Devyn being as though she was still a female. In actuality, she was more like his sister.

"Who is this broad anyway?" Ty asked, seeming the least bit interested.

Devyn sighed heavily. "Her name is Isla. We met in high school, but we got real close in college."

Ty slowed down his pace as he tiptoed into his kitchen. "Isla? I know a lil broad wit the same name. Well, I ain't seen her since back in the day. Lil orphan shorty. I swore she was fuckin wit Kalei back then." Ty spoke to himself.

Devyn shook her head. "No coincidence. We talkin bout the same bitch." She rolled her eyes. "That's the inmate I caught her wit! Kalei!"

"Oh, naw!" Ty laughed before lighting his blunt. "That's crazy as hell. Give it up. Kalei and Isla in love, been in love since we was younger," he confessed.

"Man, fuck that bitch!" Devyn shouted, slamming her fist into the countertop. "This goin be her last week. Mark my words!"

"You goin get her fired cause she fuckin that nigga? He ain't coming home no time soon, so what you complaining for? Let the bitch have her way with the both of y'all." Ty threw around his dry humor, leaving Devyn flustered.

"How the fuck you know when that nigga come home?" Devyn asked, furrowing her eyebrows.

Ty shook his head. "I said he not coming home. And I know cause I'm the reason he in there," Ty explained cheerfully as if he had done a good deed.

Devyn snapped her neck in his direction, slowly backing away. "You did what, nigga?"

Ty put his blunt to his mouth and puffed twice before blowing out the smoke. "You heard me correctly. It had to be done. Dean next." He exuded confidence in his response.

"Bruh," Devyn paused for a second, "I gotta roll off that one. I'ma holla at you."

With Draco and Kalei out the game, he automatically assumed Dean would put him in charge. Ty was careless, and when he found himself hemmed up, it was easy for him to turn on Kalei. He got close with several officers that were assigned to Dean's case and instantly put them on Kalei. He singled him out simply because he wanted him gone. Ty knew Dean was untouchable, and it would be hard to get him behind bars, let alone in cuffs. There was never enough direct evidence. He tipped Reed off and gave him the run down on all of Kalei's moves, and that was how Kalei got hemmed up - trusting the wrong person.

Ty shrugged his shoulders and smirked. "That's why he fuckin yo bitch now," he whispered under his breath.

Ty had made it clear from the jump that he was simply cooperating with the authorities to take Kalei off the map for a lesser punishment. He wasn't looking out for the interest of others; he was looking out for himself. Devyn hated even the thought of him snitching to elevate himself. She felt snitching should only be involved when the victim was defenseless or vulnerable, not in a situation like this.

"The fuck, man," Devyn whispered to herself, running her hands across her face. She hated snitches with a passion; they weren't trustworthy, and betrayal was easy for them.

"Ughhhhh!" She shouted out of frustration with several thoughts on her mental at the moment. It was hard for her to think straight.

Yale stood at the bedroom door, holding it slightly ajar, while she listened to Ty's entire conversation. Knowing the truth about what Ty had done to Kalei left a bad taste in her mouth. She knew the streets didn't know the real deal behind Kalei's arrest, or Ty would have been out the game. She quietly shut the door back and made a mental note to hit up Isla and reveal the troubling scoop she had just gotten.

Chapter 5

Brooke shoved her tongue into Ty's mouth, pushing between his lips. She kissed him with an animalistic passion, and he soon matched her aggression. His hands tangled in her hair, he bit down on her bottom lip, and it sent her crazy. Brooke placed her hands on his chest as he eased back into his seat. He wrestled with his belt, then his button, then his fly. Even though they were sitting in the parking lot of a maximum-security prison, Brooke had no hesitation. Her surroundings were irrelevant. She reached into Ty's boxers and pulled his raging penis free. He shuffled his hips and let his trousers fall past his knees. She wrapped her fingers around the base, and with her other hand, she gripped the top half of his shaft. Brooke's eyes lit up, showing a delighted amazement, before she began. She used both hands, one jerking up and down while the other ran in a twisting motion. Ty leaned back and shut his eyes. Brooke's hands felt so smooth yet so firm. He was throbbing between her fingers as he let out soft groans.

Precum began to leak from his swollen head, and Brooke noticed instantly. She ran her finger around the tip of his head, gently tracing the sticky leakage with her fingertips, then she scooped it up on her fingers. Ty watched as she took him all the way into her mouth and gave him the filthiest grin he had ever seen. Brooke's wide eyes looked up at him as she held it there, touching her tonsils. Ty could feel her throat convulsive on his head. She gagged repeatedly, allowing a flow of saliva to immediately start running down his cock. She lifted her mouth off of him as slowly as possible until his head was between her lips, then she continued to bob her head up and down again, from the tip to the base with every mouthful. Ty forceful began to push up toward her mouth and fuck her throat. She slurped and gagged and sucked on him momentarily, changing her techniques constantly, leaving Ty in ecstasy. She was so unpredictable, and he never knew what was coming next. Whenever he got used to a rhythm, she switched it up.

Brooke stopped suddenly and looked into Ty's eyes as hers were watering and glistening, a combination. Without warning, she hastily undressed herself and swung her legs over Ty, straddling him. She wasted no time guiding him inside of her; she sat straight down on top of him. Ty shuddered at the feeling of Brooke's lips swallowing him whole. What she lacked in tightness, she made up for in wetness. She began to bounce up and down. Slurping and squelching sounds were made from her juices dripping and slipping all over his throbbing manhood. Her ass cheeks slapped against his thighs every time she sat down on him. Her massive soft breasts were unescapable. Ty shoved his face into her chest, nearly suffocating himself. He felt around for her hard nipples and began to suck on them. Brooke growled as a wave of cum flowed from between her legs. She leaned back, and Ty eyeballed her perfect breasts as she rode him. She grabbed the back of his neck and made him focus on her as she grinded her hips as if she were dancing, only this time, he was inside of her. Brooke was like a fountain, and by now, Ty was lost in the moment. He began to thrust his pelvis upward to match her rhythms. Their bodies met and slammed into each other.

"Fuckkkkkk! I'm going to be late!" Isla shouted as she yanked on the wheel. Peering back and forth between the clock and the road, she attempted to dress herself while still staying in her lane. She sighed and rolled her eyes at the thought of the series of events that occurred hours prior. "Fuckin bitch," Isla thought out loud. As she realized she had been reacting off emotion, she took a moment to view the situation from Devyn's aspect. Deep down, she felt like the bad guy. All in all, she figured she could have been the bigger person instead of leading Devyn on. A girlfriend was never in her plans, but when Devyn was between her legs, things were different. Nevertheless, Kalei was back in the picture, and nothing or nobody else mattered.

Isla jammed her foot on the gas, coursing up the rugged dirt road to the facility. She found a spot instantly and put her car in park.

Damn, this a far walk, she thought to herself, shrugging her shoulders. She examined her surroundings before she got out. "What the fuck?!" she mumbled. Isla's mouth dropped, and her eyes widened as she carefully watched Brooke bounce up and down in the car directly next to her. "I know you fuckin lying." Isla gasped for air, covering her mouth with one hand. Thanking the man above for her tinted windows with front row seats, she allowed them to continue with no interruptions.

"Who the fuck is that?" Isla said to herself once more as she tried to sneak a peek at the driver.

She looked down at the time on her watch then back to the show. Impatiently, she tapped her leg, diverting her focus back and forth from the graphic sex scene next to her and the time.

"Fuck this," she whispered. Grabbing her belongings, she exited her vehicle as if her mind were somewhere else. Slamming her door shut, she switched through the rows of cars. Glancing through the windshield, she caught a glimpse of the driver. To her surprise, it was a face she knew.

Isla's mouth dropped, and she struggled to peer through the tinted windows with wide eyes. The sight of Brooke bouncing up and down caught her off guard. She instantly became overwhelmed as she tried processing it all.

The soft knock on the door indicated that her first session was about to start. The guard opened the door and escorted Kalei in then dismissed himself.

Kalei's chest heaved up and down as he caught his breath.

"You okay?" Isla questioned with a concerned look.

Kalei nodded his head and smirked. "Yeah, just finished praying and doin my daily workouts."

Isla blushed and rose her eyebrow. "Prayers? Daily workouts? I'd like to hear more." She slid on her desk and crossed her legs.

Kalei leaned back into the plush loveseat and shrugged his shoulders. "Well, I've converted to Islam," he confessed.

"Interesting. Fill me in." Isla was all ears.

"Islam is the second largest religion in the world after Christianity." He began his mini lesson. "The word Islam means "submission" or "surrender" as its faithful surrender to the will of Allah. Yeah, its roots go back further in time, but typically scholars date the creation back to the seventh century. Here we are today, the faith is spreading rapidly throughout the world. Not to mention, it's widely practiced in Africa and South Asia. They have the largest number of followers."

Isla nodded her head as she was impressed with the information he was feeding her regarding the religion he had adapted to. "So, tell me this, do you consider yourself a true Muslim man?"

Kalei nodded in approval. "I do."

"Why is that?" Isla challenged him, not wanting to accept a yes or no answer.

"The true Muslim man is just, kind, compassionate, forgiving, responsible, hardworking, humble, patient, forbearing, truthful, trustworthy, courageous, soft-hearted. I can keep going." He shrugged his shoulders and continued. "He honors women, he controls his lower desires and impulses, he fulfills the needs of others before himself, he continuously is refining his intellect, improving his character, seeking knowledge as a lifelong learner, he avoids undignified behavior and sinful deeds, he is emulating the character Prophet SallAllahu Alayhi Wa Sallam and his righteous followers to the best of his ability." He stopped to catch his breath. "I am a true Muslim man."

"When you're released, what's your plan?" Isla asked curiously.

Kalei smirked. "I plan to use my Islamic mindset and African intelligence to protect the ones I love, build a business, reclaim my wealth and status, and remain true to my beliefs," he expressed.

"I love that plan so much." Isla grinned hard, allowing a vein to show from her forehead.

"You should. You a part of it." Kalei reassured her.

"Okay, so let me get down to the nitty gritty cause I wanna know the logic behind this shit." Isla dramatically flipped her hair. "They labeled you a kingpin, and in your file, it says you been dealing inside."

Kalei shook his head and sighed with a slight grin on his face. "For starters, I'm not the kingpin. A kingpin will be almost immediately replaced by another leading criminal. What people fail to realize is that organized crime is violent, and majority of the violence is centered about the members," he explained. "Dean is the kingpin; I'm just a member. *For now,*" he emphasized.

Isla sighed and rolled her eyes. "Why do you speak so highly of him when he's the reason you're in here?"

"I'm the reason I'm here. I know right from wrong. I knew the consequences that came with my actions as well. So, this ain't on nobody but me." He took accountability as he responded. "Listen, let me break it down like this. By the time Dean became a kingpin, he was adept to criminals. He learned how to isolate himself from the majority of criminal activity and the people who worked for him performing those activities."

"So, he had other people doing his dirty work basically," Isla sassed.

"Mannn, Dean can afford some of the best defense attorneys available. How the fuck you think I'm getting released so soon? Him, he the reason." Kalei raised his voice.

Isla folded her arms and nodded. Not wanting to upset him, she changed the subject. "Okay, so, wassup witchu dealing inside? You trying to extend your sentence?"

Kalei laughed, falling back into the seat. "Draco had a proposition, and I took him up on it. That was all." He told her. "Plus, that shit four to ten times more expensive in here than it is on the street. The profits in here skyrocket for a very small amount."

Isla's mouth dropped as Kalei spilled the tea. "Are you serious right now?" The new information had been unbeknownst to her.

Kalei nodded his head. "If you can get them drugs in here, the money to be made is often well worth whatever punishment the prison can hand to a damn convict, especially the ones that's doin life or got a long sentence."

She sighed with her hand covering her mouth. "I do not get why risk it."

"Niggas wanna feed and take care of their families from prison. One of the best ways to do that is by selling drugs."

"How does it work though?" Isla pried.

"To mitigate the risks, you bring others on board while reaping the profits. Inside networking, outside connections, there will be multiple people involved which means getting things done more efficiently and effectively than one single guy trying to slang some dope," he explained.

"Let me ask you this," Isla paused, looking up to the ceiling, "you sell an addictive product that kills people. Is that not unethical to you?"

Kalei leaned forward, clasping his hands together. "Not everyone is blessed with the same advantages in life. I was born into poverty. You know this. Quitting this shit ain't an option. Most of my customers have addictions, inside and outside. I know somebody goin supply them if I don't. Nobody is forced into doing drugs. It's a free choice. So, to answer your question, no, no it is not." Kalei rose from his seat and removed his top. He walked slowly to Isla and began to undress her swiftly as their time was running out.

Kalei invaded Isla's space; pushing her shoulders back, he brushed the hair from her neck and face, looking into her eyes. He moved closer, kissing her, at first gently. But the kisses intensified, and they were firmer. His hands moved to the back of her head, tangling in her hair, pulling her into him. Kalei crushed his lips to hers, melding them together. His tongue searched her mouth like a snake. The knot of fear in Isla's stomach gradually subsided and was replaced by the intoxicating waves of desire only Kalei could arouse in her. Within no time, they found themselves out of their clothes. Kalei pushed Isla gently down on her desk. Straddling her, his rod hardened between them. His mouth had now moved to her neck, and he was licking and sucking, biting her flesh, marking his territory. But there was no need; she knew she was his.

Isla flipped over and was now dominating him. She leaned over and kissed his neck, all the while rocking her hips, massaging him. She continued her path downwards, kissing every inch of Kalei's chocolate body.

Once she reached the surface, she brought her lips to the

top of his head. Adjusting her position, she licked, hardly touching from base to tip. Kalei released a soft groan. The sound sent shivers down her spine as she opened her mouth. She slowly took all of him to the back of her throat, going deeper than she had ever dared before. She held him there for a moment, marveling at the perfect fit.

Isla drew back, using her tongue to trace back to the tip. Her fingers stroked his balls, gently massaging them. She had never felt more desperate to please him than now. She continued with long, gradual strokes, building pace. She longed to taste his cum on her tongue. One last suck pulled a low groan from Kalei as he filled her mouth. Isla licked him clean and kissed every inch of him, swallowing every drop of his delicious cum.

As she slithered up his body, Kalei flipped her over and spread her legs. He wasted no time flicking his tongue in and out of her clit. A long teasing lick from her ass to her clit drew a soft moan. Isla turned left to right, frantically looking for an object of some sort to grip on to. Kalei slightly altered the tilt of her hips, bringing his tongue in deeper. He sucked harder, tantalizingly, allowing his teeth to brush against her moist, sensitive spot. More moans forced their way from Isla's mouth, and she pushed her hips farther. He built up a rhythm while she rocked her hips gently. Kalei could feel her orgasm nearing, so he quickly got her there.

Isla dropped her head back and let out a rough scream that

echoed throughout the room. Kalei quickly covered her mouth, silencing her.

Not allowing a moment of rest, Kalei dropped her legs from his shoulders, wrapping them around his waist. In one hard, swift stroke, he slid himself in. Isla pulled him closer and closer as he moved rhythmically, fast and hard. A few ruthless thrusts took them both out. Isla's mind floated away into a world where there was only him. She listened carefully to his groans and breaths above her own. Kalei watched Isla intensely. Following the beads of sweat coursing down their bodies, Kalei sank inside of her, finally filling her with his sweet juices. The thrust continued for several more seconds until their bodies collapsed, sinking to the floor. Kalei held Isla tightly, their sweat mingling between their bodies.

Isla sighed hard before she stretched out from his grip.

"Come on, babe," she whispered. "Get dressed."

Kalei shook himself from the daydream and remembered they were still under strict supervision and now was not the time to be getting caught up.

"Wassup with lil bruh?" Kalei asked her. referring to Kannin. Chills instantly ran down Isla's spine as she thought about the sexcapade she had with Kannin. She quickly forced it to the back of her mind as if it never happened.

"He's good actually," she replied with much enthusiasm.

Kalei grinned hard and nodded. "When I come home, it's going to be the three of us again," he assured.

Isla flashed a smile back, but her insides burned. She

wanted so badly to come clean, but the fear of the unknown haunted her, and she wasn't ready to lose Kalei, at least not again. So instead, she kept her mouth shut tight and decided to take the secret to the grave with her.

"Oh, I totally forgot to tell you." Isla stood in the middle of her office, half dressed with wide eyes. She attempted to change the subject. "I saw Ty today in the parking lot."

Kalei whipped his neck in her direction but continued to dress himself before guards came knocking. "The fuck? Doing what?"

Isla shook her head. "He was fuckin the correctional officer, Brooke, in the front seat," she whispered.

"The fuck?" Kalei paused to take in the information. "That's crazy," he replied, still in deep thought.

Brooke was known to be a whore, and she did get around, but Kalei had no idea she was in bed with Ty. It had been so long since his name had even been brought up that Kalei almost forgot about his betrayal. He made a mental note of the information he received from Isla and decided to keep it to himself.

"Gimme some shugga, girl." Kalei joked, gently pulling Isla into his grasp. He planted kisses down the side of her neck, squeezing her tight. She submitted and sank into his arms, taking it all in.

"I love you, girl," he whispered in her ear, gently nibbling.

"I love you so much more, boy," Isla replied.

They could both hear the footsteps of the heavyset guard

making his way down the hall, so they knew that was their cue.

Before he could tap the door, Isla swung it open. On point, Kalei was in place and ready to be escorted back to his cell. He looked behind his shoulders and winked at Isla, causing her to blush hard.

Draco paced his tier, constantly watching the clock. When the long hand hit the number three, he took off. He glided through the halls with his head held high as he made his way to his midday appointment with his favorite person. He bumped into Brooke on the way and made a mental note of their interaction. She seemed jittery, and her eyes damn near bulged through the socket when she noticed him. "Sneaky bitch," he mumbled to himself as he watched her walk away. Since the product had been fucked up for the past couple of weeks, Draco made sure to keep his eye on Brooke. He pushed his thoughts of strangling the life out of her to the back of his head. He hit the corner, looked around to make sure he hadn't been followed or watched, then he entered. Draco slid into Rita's office excitedly. He shut the door, but in a hurry, locking it wasn't a priority. Before he could get into the office fully, Rita had invaded his space.

Rita caressed Draco's fully turgid tool, squeezing his testicles. She dropped to her knees and faced his monster as she was now just inches away. He could feel her hot breath as she snatched his sweats from his hips. Rita parted her lips and engulfed his penis into her mouth. She rolled her tongue around his pointed tip, prying him open. Draco immediately discharged a huge glob of precum into her mouth. She swirled it around inside her mouth before gulping it down like a connoisseur. Again and again, she deep throated him, taking his entire rod to the back of her palette. Draco enjoyed the warmness of her mouth. Each time she sensed his release approaching, she pinched the back of his balls, exciting him more.

Draco let out a low, deep, heavy groan from his core as he erupted into her mouth, unleashing a continuous volley of thick, rich, fresh semen that she had kept under pressure. Gobs and gobs of sperm lost themselves inside her mouth as Rita kept relentlessly sucking. Not a drop was wasted, just a trickle that oozed from the side of her lips.

"Let the festivities begin." He grinned slyly, whispering in her ear as he grabbed her from the floor. Draco found her lips and went in. The wet kiss fused them into one another; it was never ending as their tongues meshed.

Draco removed her clothing and flung it across the office.

Damn, he thought to himself. He backed away and took in Rita's beauty. She was well built, full of curves, and staring at him with a piercing gaze. Draco took in the sight fully, his cock in his hands that was now throbbing due to his enhanced excitement. He pushed Rita back onto her desk, raising her pelvis to gain maximum entry. He spread her legs as far as they would go, positioning himself at her entrance. He touched her engorged vulva with his tip and entered her with one single stroke. With his feet placed firmly, he thrusted himself into her. Draco touched her walls until he couldn't go any farther. He stayed in one spot for several seconds, enjoying the feeling of flesh with flesh. Bringing himself slowly out. he followed up with more massive thrusts, charging his tool into her uterus in full fury, slamming her as his testicles collided violently.

"Ouuuuu!" Rita groaned with pleasure to the joy Draco's stroke offered. She wailed in ecstasy each time he hammered her deeply. Their stamina matched as they both clashed into one another, meeting thrust for thrust. Draco kept at it, never once slowing down, only when he sensed his crisis approaching. But his goal was always to get Rita to reach multiple orgasms before he could discharge his release. The feeling of her bucking told him all he needed to know. Rita's entire body shook violently, quivered uncontrollably, repeatedly. She wailed helplessly and long, letting herself loose. She spewed a huge load of wetness onto his engorged penis that still happened to be inside of her. Draco continued to stroke as now it was time for him to release his pent-up desires. Pulsating with her, with a deep grunt, he released a volley of vibratory pushes and pulls. Again and again, he pummeled her pussy repeatedly, shooting inside of her.

Devyn trudged through the halls, maneuvering through the corridors with vengeance on her mind. She speed walked through the east wing, making her way to Rita. She needed to vent. On top of that, she wanted Isla gone and Kalei punished.

What a fuckin coincidence, she thought to herself as Kalei was making his way down the hall, being escorted by her colleague.

"Bitch ass nigga!" she spat, looking in his direction. She slowed, waiting for a response, but Kalei smirked and looked away.

Not receiving the reaction she had been expecting made her even angrier. She needed motive for a punishment asap. She was determined to make him suffer some way, somehow.

Fuck, Moe! she silently whispered to herself. She continued to trail down the hall. The wing had been silent, but the occasional thumping alarmed her. Without notice, she forcefully yanked the door handle, swinging it wide open; her mouth dropped instantly. *What the entire fuck,* Moe?!

Rita scrambled to find her clothing that had been strewn throughout her office, while Draco took his time. He paced the office, showing off his naked, muscular body, allowing his manhood to swing form left to right in plain sight.

"I need you to go handle them new inmates that's just been transferred. Close my damn door!" Rita shouted with frustration as she had just been caught red handed.

With wide eyes and an open mouth, Devyn slowly shut the door and did as she was told.

Frustrated, she was now in deep thought. She didn't know what to think or who to trust, let alone who to turn to in a situation like this. After Ty confessed to being a snitch last night, she wanted no parts. While he was her blood cousin, she still wanted nothing to do with a rat. Straddling the fence between pure rage and heartbreak was Isla, just lingering on her mental. She loved her wholeheartedly, and she knew deep down inside that Isla felt the same, but she couldn't pinpoint why Kalei. Having seen Rita sprawled on top of her desk left her in shock. But Draco being the enforcer made things almost more confusing for her than they already were.

What the entire fuck... Devyn sighed loudly.

Chico hopped off the transport bus with a group of thirty others who had served time before. The energy was palpable; everyone was on edge. They all peered through the steel security grates on the bus windows at the approaching menace. As the bus pulled into the parking lot, they gazed at the massive structure of concrete, steel, and spools of fencing and razor wire. Two perimeter patrol vehicles arrived with armed prison guards. They waited. The guards unlocked a fence and motioned the bus inside, locking the fence behind. A large steel door slid open, allowing the bus to pull in a vast, dimly lit garage.

Each inmate's name was called one after the other. The anxiety became an internal panic.

Once off the bus, they were thrown up against a wall and forcefully patted down.

Devyn did as she was told and chaperoned the new inmates. Each inmate was reviewed and screened by staff from the case management, medical, and mental health units. They each received formal orientations to the programs, services, policies, and procedures of the facility.

The process began with a strip search for contraband. Each inmate was required to stand before correctional officers, run their fingers through their hair, open their mouth, and squat and cough. Once the search was complete, inmates were issued the prison clothes. They were also fingerprinted, photographed, and issued an inmate identification card. They each received a bedroll consisting of two blankets, two sheets, a washcloth, a pillowcase, and a few essential hygiene items when exiting. Afterwards, each inmate was released to the open compound and directed to their housing units.

Chico wasn't a newly committed inmate; this was not his first rodeo. The bus ride was like the first day at a new school. Associations in prison could either be a strength or a downfall; he knew that from experience. Chico's goal was obscurity. He projected strength and showed that he could take care of himself, but he didn't attract too much attention or stand out.

He made his way to his unit alone. No prison guard guided him. Once he reached the intersection of the building that housed approximately one thousand inmates, the guard automatically pointed him in the right direction. Climbing the stairs to his new unit, he made his way to his cell to unpack. Chico slipped on his shoes, white tee, and khaki-colored pants, tugging on his elastic waistband. He remained calm, avoided missteps, and integrated quietly into his new home.

Chico was a menace and a minor reflection of Draco, some

say. When Draco and Kalei got booked, word on the street was that Chico had been holding shit down. Of course, that didn't last long. Chico was a hot head at heart and had no idea how to maintain his composure when it came to business. Chico was charged with a number of infractions, including murder, so that landed him with a ten-year sentence.

Chow hall was probably the most important place in the prison. Like most things, the chow hall was split up into sections based on race, states, gangs, and even the sex offenders had a section in the lows. Initially, it was good to know what section to sit in.

Once the door opened, inmates scattered throughout the room, dispersing from the single file line. The chow hall was one cavernous rectangular structure with about twenty stainless steel tables. On both sides of the dining area stood guards inside a glass cubicle pointing a rifle downward. The back of the cafe was guarded with a glass barrier separating the four convict kitchen workers.

Moving each tray along, the inmates grabbed them and used the water dispenser to pour cold water into their state issued plastic mugs.

Chico scanned the room and spotted Kalei at the front of the line.

This nigga here, Chico thought to himself. He stepped out of line and casually slid in front of Kalei. Cutting in line was a huge no, and Kalei was going to make sure Chico felt it.

He took a second to examine the individual that jumped in

front of him, but once he realized who the familiar face was, he sighed deeply, sucking his teeth.

"Go the fuck head, nigga," he whispered.

Kalei understood there were no rules in prison, just survival. There was no etiquette.

Standing a few feet away, Kalei contemplated on his next move. *Fuck it,* he thought to himself. He charged Chico instantly, causing him to throw up his forearms like an offensive lineman blocking a defensive back. Kalei stepped back, sliding to the side. He threw another swift jab which landed in Chico's face. Chico caught him back with a stiff left, which Kalei followed with a right cross. Kalei continued to slide from left to right, and he caught Chico with an uppercut right before the alarm was sounded.

Inmates gathered to watch the men showdown as they threw hands. Guards rushed the scene, stepping in between Kalei and Chico. They were ordered to separate and head back to their units.

"Bitch ass nigga," Kalei said in a low tone with a smirk on his face.

Chico and Kalei's underlying issues began their tenth-grade year of high school. Egos were in the way as well as reputations. Chico was always one that craved being the center of attention; he wanted all eyes on him at all times. That changed when Kalei popped out. Chico didn't like it; Kalei was a threat to him. But it was Draco who kept Chico in line when it came to Kalei. While he was always the strategic one, Draco never hesitated being the enforcer.

After assisting with the new inmate arrivals, Devyn wasted no time making her way to Elon. She wanted both the scoop and his word on her request. Scurrying through the corridors, she scanned the halls to make sure she hadn't been followed. She bucked a sharp left and slid into his office swiftly, shutting the door behind her.

Once inside, Elon faced her as her arms folded.

He sighed and shook his head. "What's goin on, Dev?"

"What's going on with me, or what's going on with you?" she questioned with exasperation.

Elon sighed deeply, dropping his head. "Look, I got a lot of shit goin on right now. Now is just not a good time." He slowly fell into his desk chair.

Devyn smirked and shook her head. "Listen, I thought my shit was a mess but an inmate? That shit is foul."

"The fuck are you talking about?" Elon asked, seeming uninterested.

"The fuck do you mean?" Devyn stared at him blankly, and Elon returned the stare. "Oh, shit." She covered her mouth. "You don't know. I just walked in on your wife getting beat on like a drum by an inmate," Devyn confessed.

"Oh, yeah." Elon nodded his head; he leaned back in his seat. "Is that so? What inmate?" he asked through clenched teeth.

He smoldered with resentment, and rage flowed through

him like lava. He felt a flicker of irritation, and his anger spiked instantly.

"That nigga, Draco, the lil crazy nigga that work for Dean." She filled him in.

Elon laughed. "Lil nigga ain't crazy for real. He just *act* crazy. But I got something for his ass." He glared into thin air with a sinister look in his eye. "He done met his match."

Devyn smirked, nodding her head while rubbing her hands together. "What you got in mind?" she asked with a mischievous expression plastered across her face.

"Don't worry about it. Just keep your head on a swivel." Elon made it simple and was stern with his response.

As fury tore through him, he swallowed down his frustration although he had been smoking with anger. He was already doing everything he could to get Dean out of his way, but Rita just added fuel to his fire.

Devyn rolled her eyes. "Say less but I did wanna holla at you about some other shit that you might be interested in." She changed the subject, hoping Elon would help her get Isla out the door.

Elon sucked his teeth. Dropping the files, they scattered across his desk. "Make this shit quick, man."

"Damn, I'm not worthy of your time no more?" She complained instead of getting her issue off.

"Didn't I just tell you now was not a good time?!" He slammed his fist into the desk, causing her to jump.

Devyn stood silently for seconds before she felt it was safe to speak. She causally rolled her eyes before she began. "Man, the lil bitch that had the interview."

"Isla?" He cut her off mid-sentence. "The psychiatrist?" Elon shook his head. "Not right now."

"Naw, I want that bitch gone," she pleaded. "Snatch that position right from her ass."

"Why?" Elon laughed. "Cause you in your feelings?"

"No!" Devyn pouted and folded her arms like a child. "Cause I caught the bitch fuckin an inmate, and yes, I may be in my feelings about the shit," she expressed.

Elon's smile instantly went away. "What inmate?"

"Kalei, the nigga that be with Draco," Devyn added, intentionally throwing fuel on an already lit fire.

"The fuck!" Elon slammed his fist into the desk once more. "How the fuck? Did you tell anyone else about this? Keep this shit between us, man. Don't say shit to nobody. I'll handle all of this shit," he assured her.

"Cool, say less." Devyn exited the office with her head held high with a sly grin and smirk.

Devyn hid her tears behind a sly smile. Deep down, she wanted to bawl her eyes out, but she knew now wasn't the time or place. Devyn loved Isla from her actions and simply because she believed Isla loved her back. But it was in this very moment that Devyn realized Isla didn't love her back, and she wanted to rip her own heart out, so she couldn't feel the pain any longer. She was left with tons of questions and wondering how to move on.

The sun had set, and everyone's shift was coming to an end.

Every sound echoed through the halls and tiers and blocks. Eerie silence filled the halls where the slightest sounds were amplified. There was violent slamming of the doors, and on the hour, there was the thumping sound of boots as guards did their rounds, peeping through the cracks of the cell doors. Elon crept through the halls and maneuvered through the corridors as he plotted on his next move.

In his mind, he felt as if he had been wronged, and he simply wanted to punish all perpetrators. The desire was wired within him. Revenge was a powerful force that he sought, and in exacting his revenge, he knew he'd get that form of emotional release. Retribution always made him feel better.

His nostrils flared as he paced the halls. With a hostile glare, his face was contorted with rage.

Approaching Rita's office, he roughly turned the knob, pushing the door open.

Rita jumped from behind her desk. "Ughhh, wassup, E?" She let her guard down, sighing with relief.

Elon slammed the door shut behind him. "You tell me." He shrugged his shoulders.

Rita sighed once more, falling into her seat. "Here we go with this shit." She threw her hands in the air dramatically. "What you on?"

Elon smirked and began to pace her office. "I'm on whatever you on." He toyed with her. "You the one that's fuckin inmates."

Elon was an emotional wreck and known to let his feelings be the main input to a decision as opposed to analyzing it rationally. Elon was the type to act impulsively.

"Excuse me!?" Rita rose to her feet and challenged Elon, knowing there was truth behind his words.

"Bitch, don't act dumb!" He snapped. "You know what the fuck I'm talking about! The real question is how long you been fuckin that nigga, Draco, behind my back?" Elon grilled her with a piercing stare, filled with jealousy and rage.

Rita stood in silence and shrugged her shoulders carelessly after not having a comeback. "The fuckin nerve of you to call me out like you ain't been doing your dirt too," she sassed.

"That's besides the fucking point!" Elon raised his hand, silencing her.

"Nigga, please! Matter of fact, fuck you! And I'm goin keep fuckin who I wanna fuck as long as you continue to do the same." Rita reached across her desk, tapping him on the nose; she antagonized him.

Elon smirked. "Is that right?" He nodded his head. Running his hands over his face, he flexed his jaw muscles. "You really think I'm goin let that shit fly? You really think I'm goin let this shit right here slide?" He extended his pointer finger, reaching her forehead. "Bitch, you crazy. You mine! You belong to me!"

Rita giggled. "That's your problem right there. You're so

fuckin entitled. That's where you go wrong. I'm done with this shit."

Elon nodded his head; he tiptoed his way behind her desk.

Smack!

He quickly rose his hand and whacked her across the face, causing her to stumble and hit the ground instantly from the blow.

Rita staggered, trying to find her balance. "Bitch, you ain't done til' I say you done." Elon grabbed her by the hair and forcefully shoved her across to the opposite side of the room.

Nearly suffocating on fury, he drowned himself in his own anger. Instead of striking her once more, he turned on his heels and headed for the door.

"Fuck that bitch," he whispered under his breath but loud enough for Rita to hear him.

Once Isla clocked out and made herself at home, it was always a wrap. There was nothing she enjoyed more than time to herself and a tall glass of wine after work. Sade's *Sweetest Taboo* echoed throughout the home, and Isla danced along to the song. Kannin had stopped past to shower and redress. Isla allowed him to do so, but she made sure she stayed as far away as possible, especially after the last time they happened to be alone together. Isla spun around in circles and gyrated through her entertainment room. One hand was on her hip and the other occupied with her wine glass.

Yale let herself in. Trudging up the steps, she caught Isla

doing the Dutty Wine. Isla did a three sixty spin, catching Yale out of her peripheral.

"Unt unt, don't come round here wit your face screwed up, bitch. I'm in a good mood," she slurred.

Yale smirked. "I see. Why so chipper?" she asked dryly.

"I've reunited with the love of my life, and it feels so good," she blurted out. "And what's so crazy to me is that back then, we were both scared to admit it. But I love that man deeply," she expressed.

Yale rose her eyebrow, slightly confused. "Hold the fuck up." She threw her hands in the air. "Kalei? Where the fuck you reunite with Kalei at?"

Isla shrugged her shoulders. "You're looking at the new psychiatrist at Lorton Correctional Facility," she joyfully announced. "Butttt, there was this girl I was real tight with. She wanted a relationship, but I didn't, ya know, and then Kalei was there. I had to just shut it down," Isla rambled.

"The fuck? You was fuckin wit a girl?" Yale stared at Isla in awe. "This is too much to take in."

"I'm sorry. I just put all that on you without really going into detail. I just had to let it out." She spoke with slurred speech. "The bitch came through last night while Kannin and I was on the couch knocked the fuck out." She left out the part where she fucked Kannin like he was Kalei.

"And she automatically though y'all was fuckin." Yale cut her off, finishing her sentence.

Isla nodded. "Kannin told that bitch she had to roll. Her

mad ass left my spare key and some more shit. I wasn't mad at all though."

Yale shook her head and laughed hysterically. "Ughhh, this explains it all. What a small world. I came to holla at you about some shit I just found out."

"Good or bad?" Isla rolled her eyes.

"Very bad," Yale whispered, balling her face up. "Remember that nigga, Ty, that used to hang with Kalei and Draco a few years back?"

Isla nodded as she began to have flashbacks of Brooke bouncing up and down in the driver's seat and Ty being the driver. "Yeah, what about him?"

"Well, it was said that he started doing his own thing when they got booked. Long story short, I started fuckin with Ty behind Draco back," Yale confessed.

As Isla was tilting her glass back, she spit her wine out. "The fuck, Yale? You playing a dangerous game."

Yale sucked her teeth. "Listen, the dick was immaculate, okay? Too good to give up, ya hear me?"

Isla shook her head in disappointment. "This bitch fuckin the members," she whispered.

"Look, last night was the first time I heard him admit it. Everybody was weary and assumed he had snitched, but nobody could prove it. But some broad came through last night, Kalei name was brought up, and Ty specifically said, 'I'm the reason that nigga in there,' and I almost fell out, bitch." Yale dramatically placed her hand across her forehead as if she were about to faint.

"Was she a correctional officer? Brooke?" Isla chimed in.

"Unt unt, what the fuck that bitch got to do with this?" Yale's mood changed in an instant.

Isla shrugged her shoulders. "Ion know. I just figured she was the broad you was referring to. Because I kind of caught them fuckin in the car earlier before her shift." Isla dropped the ball.

Yale stared at Isla in awe once again. "I know you fuckin lying."

Isla shook her head. "May the Lord strike me down if I'm lying." She looked up to the ceiling then back at Yale seconds later.

"That just threw me off." Yale turned up her nose and poured herself a glass of wine since Isla never offered her a cup.

She threw it back, wasting no time. She took big gulps.

Isla sat in silence as she ventured down memory lane. "Wow, so Ty is the reason Kalei got locked up that night, huh? I'll never forget that shit."

Kannin, still a bit damp, tiptoed to the door that had been ajar and pressed his ear against it. He just listened. His jaws were clenched tight as were his fists. His adrenaline began to thump. He wrapped his towel around his lower body and descended the stairs quietly. Kannin stood tucked behind the accent wall near the kitchen. He listened but said nothing.

Instead, he pulled out his Smith and Wesson and tiptoed into the kitchen.

"I'll never forget that night either." His voice traveled through the kitchen just as the bullet did. He squeezed the trigger and watched the bullet punch through the back of Yale's head and exit through the front. She hit the floor in an instant.

Isla stood, frozen.

Isla found the nearest wall and used it for support. She steadied her breathing and attempted to calm the panic, but she was paralyzed by the menacing aura holding her in a tight grip. Terror sucked the very breath from her mouth, washing over her, raising the fine hairs on her neck. Due to the loud ring, her pulse was beating in her ears, blocking out all other sounds.

Kannin's smug facial expression spoke a thousand words. He paced Isla's small dining area, careful not to contaminate the scene. He trudged back and forth, peering through the window. He had already made the call to Dean that shit was going down. He was simply awaiting his arrival.

Impatiently, he continued to pace from one side of the room to the other, becoming jittery.

Kannin stood over top of Yale's body for several seconds. After he pulled the trigger, he felt a mix of emptiness and rage. He also felt regret, but that was only until part of his brain chimed in, reminding him that they were the bad guys. After that, he didn't feel anything anymore.

"It had to be done," he whispered in Isla's direction but never acknowledged her.

Isla, still planted in place, stared down at Yale's lifeless body and the hole that pierced her skull.

"Kannin, what the fuck?" she whined softly. "There is a dead body on my fuckin floor." She trembled at the sight.

Kannin shrugged his shoulders and tuned her out. "You'll be iight."

The flashing lights beamed through her curtains suddenly, and Kannin sprinted through the home, skipping down the flight of steps. He wasted no time snatching the door open. Instantly, he was greeted.

"Head up and get started." Dean moved aside and allowed his cleaners to enter the home first. They were the best in the game. In fact, Dean kept them on call for incidents of all sorts. "Let me holla at you." He directed his attention to Kannin.

Kannin stepped to the side, and Dean entered, stopping at the bottom step. "The fuck happened?" he asked, puzzled.

Kannin shrugged his shoulders. "I clipped that bitch," he began. "She came over here, gossiping and shit, talkin bout how she been fuckin the nigga, Ty, and he snitched on my brother!" Kannin explained with tears in his eyes.

Dean nodded his head but didn't say much; instead, he let his thoughts take control. "Oh, yeah?"

"Yeah, the nigga was braggin' bout it and shit, kept sayin' he was the reason my brother locked up." Kannin paused to take a breath. "Man, I had to get the bitch up outta here, and I'm goin handle Ty bitch ass." He assured.

"Naw, you lay low, baby boy," Dean demanded. "I'll handle that shit."

Kannin shook his head defiantly. "Naw, D. It needs to be me. That's my brother."

"This shit ain't on you, lil bro. Try not to beat yourself up about it too much." Dean patted him on the chest. "Don't make this shit your burden. Ty goin get dealt with." He reassured him.

Kannin threw his hands up in defeat. "Okay, you got it. Say less." He sighed and rolled his eyes, allowing his attitude to say otherwise.

Dean shook his head and proceeded up the steps. "Let me go holla at Isla. I know the girl head probably all fucked up."

"Ion know what the fuck you did to her, but she ain't feelin' your ass." Kannin stopped him on his way up to fill him in.

Dean smirked. "That's because she doesn't know me."

Dean crept through Isla's home uninvited. He took note of the scene and watched as his cleaners took care of the mess. Kannin stood in the corner with revenge on his mind as Dean made his way over to Isla. She had backed herself into the wall and slid down to the floor. She shook frantically, rocking back and forth with her knees pulled into her chest.

Dean kneeled down beside her. "Everything is handled, Isla, and when the time is right, we can talk." He spoke sincerely with a serene tone that somewhat soothed her, but not enough. Isla broke her stare and blinked a few times before she jumped up from the floor.

"This is fuckin insane," she whispered under her breath. She trudged through her home, careful not to slip and fall on the dead body or the pool of blood that was currently seeping into her floors. She stomped through her entertainment room and darted up the stairs to her bedroom. Slamming the door shut, she locked it behind her.

"What the fuck?!" she shouted and began sobbing. Isla dropped to the floor, but within seconds, she realized what the common denominator had been.

"It's Kannin," she said to herself.

Chapter 6

As soon as Kalei opened his eyes, he got himself ready for Fajr Salah, his morning prayer. The Fajr Salah was the first of the five obligatory Muslim prayers of the day. Kalei started at dawn and finished at sunset. He began with his prayer intentions before he started. Kalei stood up and faced the Qibla as he performed his intention. While standing up right facing the direction of Al-Ka'bah, he started the prayer. He did two sets of rakat and ended the prayer.

Visiting hours were from 8 to 3 p.m., so Kannin made sure he arrived at six to spend as much time as he possibly could with Kalei. Kannin skipped into the facility, sliding through the metal detectors. He flashed his ID at the stalky guard behind the desk and kept it moving. He added some money to his card for his trips to the vending machines and skimmed the tiny room until he found a seat in the waiting area.

"Bitch ass nigga." Devyn made sure she was heard when they crossed paths.

Kannin snapped his neck before turning his body to face her direction. "Bitch, wassup witchu?" He had stopped following the guard and decided to put on the show. "Talkin real heavy cause we in your place of work. I'll smash you, bitch!" He threatened in a harsh tone.

"Sir, you're gonna have to go if you continue with this behavior." The guard intervened. "Come this way. Ignore her." She continued to escort Kannin into the visitation area.

Stupid bitch, he thought to himself.

Devyn smirked and continued to walk with her hands resting on her belt.

Kannin couldn't visit Kalei often, but he came when he could. He entered the visitation area, found a table, and made himself comfortable in the plastic chair. Kalei emerged from the back within seconds, all smiles. Visitations made his day, especially when the visits were from a loved one. He rushed the table, and Kannin stood and allowed Kalei to pull him in for a tight hug.

"Wassup, lil nigga?" Kalei greeted him with a huge grin. He studied Kannin and noticed they were more alike than he figured. Kannin was laid back, soft spoken, and hard to read. Kalei couldn't tell what he had on his mind because Kannin's facial expression had been bare, just like his.

Kannin giggled partially. "Ain't shit. Wassup, bruh?" He dapped him up.

"Look at you, holding shit down I heard." Kalei clasped his hands together and nodded his head in approval.

Kannin grinned slyly, slowly nodding his head. "You know me, bruh."

"That's iight. That's what I like to hear." Kalei leaned back in the chair, folding his arms. He was proud.

"I miss you, man," Kannin expressed.

"I'll be home before you know it," Kalei responded cheerfully.

"We goin be running this shit together." Kannin winked at him. "I can't fuckin wait!"

"You hear me doe!"

"Heard Isla back." Kannin changed the subject. "Y'all getting back?"

Kannin tested the waters, still hesitant on bringing their little encounter up. Truth be told, it was an accident, but he'd be lying if he said he didn't enjoy it. He'd actually be lying if he said he didn't want more.

"Yeah, that's my baby. I'm glad she's back." Kannin noticed Kalei's tone and expression softened when Isla was brought up. "And I'm bout to come home. This shit is perfect, man."

"That's wassup." Kannin forced a smile. "Fam back together finally."

Kalei got silent as he fell into a daze thinking about Isla and their future.

"But look though," Kannin interrupted. "I gotta holla at you about something."

Kalei took note of the concerned look on Kannin's face. "I'm all ears." He scooted closer to the table, indicating that he wanted him to keep his voice down.

"I clipped that lil bitch, Yale," he confessed.

"What?!" Kalei whispered.

Kannin nodded and shrugged his shoulders. "Broad came over to holla at Isla about that nigga, Ty, you and Draco used to run with. According to her, she overheard him talking to some lil bitch," Kannin explained. Kalei leaned back and wondered if it was Brooke he had been referring to, but he continued to take it all in. "He told the bitch he ratted you out, bruh."

Kalei smirked and laughed. "I know, I knew, and I been knew."

"I'm goin handle that for you." Kannin assured with a stern tone.

"Naw, *you* not. I am," Kalei clarified.

Kannin sucked his teeth, falling back in his seat. "The fuck? You goin get released, do some nut shit, and end up right back in here?"

"Well, what the fuck I look like letting my little brother handle my shit?" Kalei shot back. "Kannin, I said what I said. Don't do nothing stupid!"

"Say less, bro." Kannin threw his hands up in defeat and nodded.

Draco skipped through the corridors, wide eyed, with a smile plastered across his face. He strutted up and down the halls with his head held high as if he was the man. Hitting the east wing of the building, he made his way to Rita's office.

Love was not up Draco's alley, but he insisted on calling it that when it came to Rita. In the beginning, he only experienced the small things - a faster heartbeat, sweating, and even blushing. But gradually, he found himself constantly thinking about her, daydreaming, and imagining a future with her. In a sense, he was also somewhat sprung. Draco was infatuated with Rita, and no one else seemed to matter quite as much as she did.

"Inmate! Where do you belong?" a correctional officer shouted down the hall.

Draco snapped his neck in her direction. Shaken from his thoughts, he waved her off, sucking his teeth. Rita could hear the guard in her office, and within seconds, Draco was bursting through the door.

"Sup, lova?" He greeted Rita but was quickly interrupted by the guard.

"Good morning, Warden. I apologize. He beat me to the door." She explained herself.

Rita nodded and waved the guard off. "It's fine. I told him to come see me around this time," Rita objected, siding with Draco against her better judgement.

He smirked with folded arms, casually shrugging his shoulders as the guard showed herself out.

Rita turned from left to right in her desk chair, occasionally fidgeting with her hair. Her goal was to cover the bruises Elon intentionally left.

"Wassup, Moe? Why you so jittery?" Draco examined her from the opposite side of the desk.

Rita shrugged her shoulders, keeping her hand covering her face. "We goin have to cut this shit out," she confessed.

Draco smirked. He sauntered toward her, but Rita jumped up from behind her desk, pushing him away.

"The fuck?!" Draco whipped Rita's hair behind her ear and saw red.

Draco's silence spoke volumes. He lunged in Rita's direction, forcefully grabbing her face to examine her wounds. The bruising had darkened to a shade of blue, purple, and black, causing the blood to leak into the top layer of her skin. "Draco, I need you to calm down in this office." Rita tried to reason with him in a stern tone.

He went cold with fury; he almost choked on his rage. His frustration kicked in immediately, and he wanted blood. He was a pure ball of anger waiting to be unleashed.

Draco sucked his teeth and began to pace her office. He ran his hands down his face and sighed heavily.

"Fuck, Moe!" he shouted once more, slamming his fist into the wall. "That nigga done. I promise you that."

Rita scurried to his side. Gripping his chest, her eyes

widened but softened. "D, baby, relax. He ain't worth it. And me and him are done."

"Then what the fuck is the issue, Rita? Why the fuck you just tell me we goin have to cut the shit? You playin' games and shit now." Draco challenged her.

"D, I don't know what the fuck to do," she expressed teary eyed, not knowing her next move, let alone how to move forward.

Draco nodded and headed for the door. "Don't even fuckin worry about it, Ri. It's done." He shot her a menacing glare, slamming the door behind him.

Isla paced her office and cursed herself for allowing Kannin to kill Yale. She didn't even know his exact reason, and he still hadn't managed to reach out with an apology either. Isla sucked her teeth as she ran her fingers through her hair. "Fuck, fuck, fuck!"

Frightened by his entrance, she jumped.

Draco was running on sheer anger as fury twisted inside of him.

"What the..." she whispered to herself but let her guard down when she realized it had been Draco.

Isla's quick and uneasy breathing caused her heart rate to accelerate. Her palms began to sweat, and she didn't know what to expect by Draco's body language. Draco didn't bother knocking. Instead, he stormed through the door, knocking Isla off her A game.

"Fuckkkk, Moe!" He shouted, falling into the seat that had been tucked in the corner. He folded his arms, and flexing his jaw, he shook his head. "I need to talk."

Isla nodded her head. "I'm listening." Her voice cracked.

Draco shook his head, tapping his foot uncontrollably. "I'm in love, Isla. I really love this woman."

"Then what's the issue?" Isla's eyes began to water as she assumed he had been referring to Yale.

"Her husband, the prison shit, it's so much in the way," he expressed. "I don't know what to do at this point. I know for a fact I ain't getting out no time soon. I mean, there's a possibility, and I have a shot but..."

"But what? And who the fuck are you referring to? Since when was Yale married?" Isla questioned him. "Yale is dead," Isla whispered, teary eyed, not knowing how Draco would react.

He waved off her comment and shrugged his shoulders. "Yale knew what the fuck she got herself into when she started fuckin that nigga." He began to vent. "She been fuckin him since I got sentenced, and that was way back. Grimy ass bitch!" he spat.

Isla, wide eyed, was shocked but not too surprised.

"She started fuckin the nigga that snitched on my right-hand man. To make it even worse, the bitch knew we was friends at one point. So, I don't blame lil bruh for clippin' her ass," he confessed with hate in his eyes. "Yale was my baby, but the bitch wasn't loyal."

Isla let out a deep sigh of relief, but her heart still ached for Yale. Though they weren't the best of friends, they were cordial and had a past beginning in high school.

Draco smirked. "Rita. I'm talking about the warden."

Isla dropped her jaw. Standing in silence, she cautiously tiptoed to her seat. "Nigga, you fuckin the warden?"

Draco continued to smirk; he shook his head. All in all, his silence told Isla exactly what she needed to know.

"How long?" she pried.

Draco shrugged his shoulders. "A cool lil while, long enough to not allow no nigga to put his hands on her. That shit ain't goin cut it," he stated harshly.

"Who been putting their hands on her? You talkin in circles. I'm so confused." Isla grabbed her head. "Start from the beginning."

Draco shook his head. "Nah, long story short, I'm goin dead that nigga."

"Bro, I need you to relax," Isla coached. She reached across, grabbing his hand, and she squeezed it. "You're bout to come home soon. Don't let nobody on the inside fuck that up for you."

A hard knock caused Isla to release her grip. She stood to her feet as the guard swung the door open.

"Warden wants to see you in the East Wing in ten

minutes." The guard delivered the message and went on his way.

Draco sucked his teeth and pouted. He sat in deep thought for seconds as he thought about both the impossible and the real world.

A combination of dread and anxiety took over all at once as Isla followed behind Rita. Rita bent the hall, and Isla followed behind her toward the west wing of the prison. Entering the conference room, Isla was face to face with the board members.

"Good morning, Ms. Harrison!" Elon shouted across the room, making sure he had her full attention. "Well, afternoon I should say." He snuck a peek at his watch.

The conference room was neutral and business oriented, outfitted with a board table. The color on the walls set the tone for the atmosphere, which happened to be calm and douche colors, promoting focus and relaxation.

The vibe was off, and Isla could sense it. It was as if there was a looming argument or a nerve competition. The tension in the air was almost palpable.

The Bureau of Prisons was a massive bureaucracy, organized under the executive branch of government. As the leader of the Department of Justice, the attorney general appointed a director to lead the bureau. The director operated from the headquarters in the DC office, also known as the "Central Office." Administrators who worked in the office presided over an organization with more than two hundred and fifty thousand employees. The reginal director presided over each of the institutions and employees in his region. Fortunately, Dean had the director in his back pocket. It was, in turn, how Elon was granted the job. Now here he was, jeopardizing his career because his emotions were in the way.

"Uhh, good morning," Isla mumbled as she studied the room as well as the people that were in attendance.

"Have a seat," Rita whispered.

"What is this about if you don't mind me asking?" Isla asked, her voice cracking.

Elon smirked. "We recently learned a few new things about you within the past twenty-four hours." He joked. "So, how about you tell us?"

Elon stood in the corner while his peers sat facing her. Isla stared at the board then back to Elon blankly. She shrugged her shoulders.

"It's been brought to our attention that you've been engaging in sexual intercourse with the inmates."

"Excuse me?" Isla frowned, denying the accusations that she knew to be true.

"No need to deny it. We simply brought you here to inform you of your termination," Elon stated. "And don't worry. We'll draft everything up for you in writing as well. Believe me when I say this is such a shame, Ms. Harrison. You just started, and I had high hopes for you."

A board member agreed, nodding her head. "Likewise, the inmates' feedback has been remarkable. I'm confused."

"There must be a misunderstanding." Isla rose to her feet as she began to defend herself.

"Actually, there is." Dean interjected as he entered the room. He sauntered and paced back and forth. "Good afternoon, everyone. Apologies for my absence and late arrival."

"A decision has already been made based on the underlying factors." Elon cut him off.

"And what might those be?" Dean challenged him. "And why was a decision made without me being present? That is not how we work around here. Furthermore, I've spoken with a dozen of the inmates, and according to my findings, Ms. Harrison's dealings with inmates has been nothing but a rumor," Dean explained.

The board quickly diverted their focus to Elon then back to Dean. "This type of thing happens often with new female employees."

"I agree." Another board member sided with Dean.

Elon shook his head. "I'm sure we can all agree to disagree, but a decision has already been made," he argued.

"Without any hard evidence that shows Ms. Harrison engaging in these activities, we cannot simply just let her go." Dean went against him once more.

"Agreed, that would be unjust on our behalf," a board member replied. "And like I mentioned before, the feedback I have been getting has been fantastic."

"I would say keep up the good work and stay out the way,"

a lead board member stated right before kicking his feet up on the desk. "You see where you are now."

"Warden, do you have anything to add?" Dean turned to Rita, who had been covering her bruises.

This bitch better not say shit, Isla thought to herself. *Especially not after what Draco just told me.*

She shook her head. "No, not at the moment; I don't. The therapist is fine with me."

Everyone in attendance nodded as they had come to an agreement, with the exception of Elon, who stood in the corner with his lip poked out and face screwed up. "Okay, well, Ms. Harrison, we wholeheartedly apologize and hope this doesn't affect you here at the facility in the near future."

Isla nodded but kept her comments to herself. "Thank you. I appreciate it. Things happen. I'm just grateful it was all able to be cleared." She shot a piercing glare at Elon, who returned the gesture.

"Thank you for your time, Ms. Harrison."

"I'll show you out." Dean extended his hand after opening the door, showing Isla out.

The two made their way down the hall in silence. Once they turned the corner, Isla slopped in her tracks, and she faced him.

"Uh, what the fuck was that?" she sassed, folding her arms. "Look, I appreciate you, but I don't need you. I ain't Kalei."

Dean smiled and shook his head. "That's a damn shame. I

just saved your ass back there. They wasn't goin hesitate to get you up outta here either."

Isla rolled her eyes. Sighing loudly, she ran her hands through her hair. "Devyn," she whispered.

"What about her?" Dean asked in a concerned tone.

"This shit was all her." Isla paced the hall. "She's the one who caught me and Kalei. She overheard us."

Dean nodded. He leaned against the wall. "Makes sense. More than likely, she told Rita or my brother."

"My bet is your brother. He got it out for me for some odd reason." Isla pointed down the hall as she had been referring to the meeting.

"I wouldn't put it past his foul ass," he interjected.

"And Rita," Isla paused to stop and roll her eyes. "I'm glad she kept her mouth shut. Cause I'm sure that bitch ain't want me to let the board know she fuckin Draco just like I'm fuckin Kalei."

"Say what?" Dean's eyes widened as this was new news to him.

"Look, forget I told you that." Isla brushed her comment off. "I'm fuckin up client privilege."

Dean smirked and shook his head once more. He was beginning to grow fond of Isla even though he could sense that she still somewhat despised him. "Well, look," he began to walk again, "you straight for now. Just stay out the way from here on out."

While she was grateful, there was still an ick about Dean

she couldn't shake. In her world, he was the bad guy. He was the reason Kalei was taken from her, and she hated him for it. Isla honestly believed that if Kalei never got involved with Dean, things would have turned out differently for the both of them. That was until she recalled life with Moe as a child and realized that they were shut out of luck to start with. But it was the sincerely and genuineness that Kalei exuded when he spoke about Dean. In a sense, Dean saved Kalei. It was not the way Isla would have preferred, but he took him in and put him under his wing. She didn't know much about him besides what the streets had to say, but she figured he couldn't have been that bad, or he put on a damn good facade. She didn't know Dean's story, nor did she know him well enough to continue to hold a grudge, so for now, she decided to let her guard down.

Isla nodded and observed her surroundings. "Where you are taking me?" she asked, studying the unknown area.

"To Kalei," he replied, making his way to the chow hall. He pushed past the heavy double doors, and Isla followed behind. Dean maneuvered through the room until Isla caught Kalei out of her peripheral.

"He's all yours." Dean extended his hands and turned on his heels.

"Thank you, Dean." Isla turned to make sure she caught him before he made an exit.

Dean nodded. "Anytime, Isla." His deep voice managed to stretch across the room.

Kalei snatched Isla into the closet and shut the door. The

tiny closet was big enough for a deep sink with a few shelves that lined the wall, along with materials and storage equipment. As it was built into the wall, it gave them a bit of space. While it wasn't opulent, it was still functional and did its best. Kalei snatched Isla gently by the waist and pulled her in close. He buried his face in her neck and began to plant kisses.

"See, he ain't as bad as he seems, is he?" Kalei asked, still holding her tightly.

"I guess not." Isla shrugged her shoulders. "I mean, he did just save my job."

Kalei laughed. "Yeah, word travels fast around here. Heard Devyn bitch ass was pushing for you to get your job snatched," he explained. "Elon set the whole meeting up."

Isla's mouth dropped. "Are you serious?"

In surprise, her eyes widened, and her jaw dropped open as if a sudden jolt of electricity had coursed through her veins, leaving her stunned in the moment.

Kalei sucked his teeth. "Look, boo, this shit politics, nothing personal."

"Babe, this is very personal." Isla disagreed with him. "All of it."

"All of what?" Kalei questioned with a puzzled look.

Isla sighed, shrugging her shoulders. "Yale is dead, and it's just..."

Kalei cut her off. "I know. I heard, boo." Kalei ran his hands through her hair and gently massaged her back.

"What?" Isla raised her tone. "Heard how?"

"Relax. Kannin came up for a visit this morning and filled me in on everything," he confessed. "It's all good. You straight, he straight, we straight. It's done and over with. Nothing is coming back to bite you in the ass." He assured her. "I just need you to relax."

Isla sighed, letting her guard down. "Nigga, we in a pantry closet, and you want me to relax?" She joked, crossing her arms.

Kalei released her from his grip, backing up as much as he could. He began to undress himself; Isla followed suit.

Kalei roughly grabbed Isla by her head and shoved his tongue in her mouth. It had been so long, and his lips and tongue tasted incredible to her. They both began to moan into each other's mouth very softly yet passionately.

He finished undressing her with a quickness without breaking a kiss. Sliding her shirt down, he broke the kiss and was surprised to see his favorite twins. His fingertips traced all over Isla's upper body, from her neck to her shoulders. She started to shake in intervals in Kalei's arms.

The faint light crept from under the door. Kalei pinned her to the wall, and gently lifting her, he placed her on the shelf. Slowly, he removed her bottoms, placing himself in between her legs. Their breaths were getting heavier and hotter. Isla could feel his hard cock rubbing her inner thigh. Kalei brushed his finger across her nipples, and her panties soaked at that moment. She took note of the lusty grin on his face. Kalei took one nipple in his mouth at a time, and Isla dropped her head back with her eyes shut tightly. He enjoyed nibbling on her erect nipples.

Isla wrapped her legs around his waist. She could feel Kalei's hands softly roaming her lower body. Kalei ceased, and backing up, he pulled himself out. Isla grinned slyly, letting out soft moans. Kalei invaded her space, pushing her panties to the side. In an instant, he inserted himself and went to pound town. He had directly hit her g-spot, causing her to convulse back-to-back. She shook uncontrollably, shivering. Without removing himself, he gently gripped Isla, lifting her in the air. He slowly guided her up and down on his hard shaft. As Isla requested him to go deeper, Kalei fulfilled her request. He could feel her juicing as he planted kisses on her neck. He kept pounding for several more seconds until he shot his load inside of her. Isla hugged him tightly, locking her legs around his body. After a long kiss, they knew that they had to go their separate ways.

Dean crept into Rita's office with a smirk on his face, already knowing what to expect. Without a greeting, Elon was on him before he stepped foot in the door.

"What the fuck is up with you undermining me in my place of business?" Elon shouted with frustration.

Rita dropped her head back and allowed herself to spin around in the desk chair. Dean stared at Elon blankly, maintaining his composure. He then turned to Rita who had clearly been hiding what he could see now.

"Damn, Ri, what happened to your face?" Dean asked,

knowing the culprit was in the room. Rita sat in silence. Instead, she continued to spin around, ignoring the sibling rivalry.

"Damn, bruh, you can't find anybody on your level to go toe-to-toe with? That's fucked up." Dean shook his head, antagonizing Elon as he knew he would receive a reaction.

Elon sighed lightly. "I need you to leave." He pointed to the door.

Dean chuckled. "Nigga, excuse me?" He paused where he stood and folded his arms. "You know who the fuck you talkin to? Remember who got you this fuckin job. Humble yourself."

Rita smirked and nodded her head at Dean's remark.

"Fuck you!" Elon spat with rage.

"No, nigga, fuck you!" Dean replied. "You need to tighten up. Man, the fuck up, soft ass nigga," he chastised. "I need you to come correct before I strip you of this position that got you feeling all high and mighty. The same way you tried to do with Ms. Harrison, which was a complete failure by the way," he added. "How the fuck you goin bring something to the board with no proof? Nigga, make it make sense."

"I tried to tell him," Rita interjected but was cut off by Dean.

"Her fuckin Kalei ain't no worse than your bitch fuckin Draco." Dean dished out the tea, and Rita gasped for air. "Yeah, I know about your wild ass."

"Fuck this shit. I'm gone." Elon stormed out of the office, leaving the door wide open.

Dean smiled hard and proceeded to push the door shut. Rita dropped her head on her desk and sighed before falling back into her seat and staring at the ceiling.

"He despises you, D," she whispered.

Dean shrugged. "I'm sure he does. I'm what he will never be, and the sooner he gets that through his head, there will be no more beef. Since a jit, a motherfucker can't compete where he don't compare," he expressed.

Rita shook her head. "It's deeper than that."

Dean folded his arms and sighed. "How much deeper, Ri? Fill me in. I already know my brother hates me. This ain't nothing new. With him, it's always how he goin try to fuck me over, ruin my reputation, or something of that sort." He shrugged his shoulders. "But I'm always one step ahead, and that's why he hates me so much. He can't beat me or be me."

"Make sense I guess." Rita considered his reasonings. "He hates you; so therefore, he hates Draco and Kalei. That's why he was so hell bent on getting Isla fired. But as far as what he had in store for them, I'm not sure what he got planned."

Dean nodded and began to pace the office in silence in deep thought. "He tryin fuck up my money. That's his game plan. He knows, for a fact, Draco and Kalei are my money makers. They're key players in my operation behind the walls; that's what he's after. He knows if he fuck them over, my money will plummet." Dean put things into perspective.

"Well," Rita kicked her feet up on her deck with a smug expression, "I suggest you get him before he gets to you first."

"Oh, don't worry. This shit is chess. His slow ass only knows about checkers, hence to why he's in the predicament he's in now."

They both burst into laughter. "Y'all is something else."

"Naw, for real, all bullshit aside, I love you to death, Ri... always and forever. I don't care what you got goin on with E or Draco. That's your business," he stated. "But when I say you goin always have a place in my heart, I mean that." He assured. "Do not let no nigga raise their hand to you ever again." Dean invaded her personal space, speaking through clenched teeth. He made sure he got his point across. "And if you're ever in need, do not hesitate to call my phone. I don't care what we going through. Do you understand?"

Dean and Rita had always been the best of friends, even when she decided to fuck on his brother. His loyalty to her never changed, and he remained the same. He always had a soft spot for Rita. While he didn't want any relations, he still didn't want to see her in a predicament such as the one she was in.

Rita nodded with teary eyes. She let them fall instead of wiping them away. "I got you, D." She sobbed quietly. "I appreciate you."

Dean nodded and made an exit.

Headed to population, Dean marched down the hall, approaching Kalei and Draco. They had their own spot to hang when they weren't in their cells and in the yard.

"Wassup wit y'all niggas?" Dean asked, wanting to receive his update on anything they felt was necessary for him to hear.

Kalei shook his head and shrugged his shoulders. "Ain't shit."

"Aye, D, let me holla at you bout something," Draco said with an intense stare. Dean smirked and gave Draco the floor. "You'd be mad if I killed your brother?" he asked honestly.

Dean smirked, shaking his head. "Of course not." He flashed teeth. "But I plan on getting to him first. But I need y'all niggas to relax and focus on this paper. Y'all bout to be outta here sooner than later," he preached.

"Nah, bruh." Draco shook his head, unsatisfied with Dean's answer.

"This about E putting his hands on Rita?" Dean dropped his head and laughed lightly. "Listen, my nigga, that shit ain't goin happen no more. Furthermore, she should be the least of your concern. We ain't worried bout no pussy, nigga. We on money." Dean took his pointer finger and tapped him in the head.

"Give us the green light when you ready, on your terms," Kalei emphasized.

Dean nodded and walked off.

"Fuck that shit, bruh. We goin get Chico out the way, then handle Elon bitch ass." Kalei rubbed his hands together, assuring Draco everything would come in due time.

Things had been crazy over the past few days, and Brooke had been at the center of it all. She was a good fuck but not to be trusted. Kalei had started piecing together his own puzzle in his mind and had come to the conclusion that Brooke was involved without a doubt, and nothing was coincidental. Kalei and Draco headed back to their unit and schemed until she made her grand appearance.

Brooke switched through the corridors, making her way to the pods to conduct her rounds. Draco quickly swung his cell door open. He rushed behind her, covering her mouth. He then proceeded to drag her back into the cell.

As she resisted, Draco finally released his grip once inside.

"Draco, what the fuck?!" Brooke shouted as she looked around to make sure she wasn't in harm's way. "Wassup, Kalei?" She looked his way, but he ignored her greeting.

"Wassup witchu, Brooke?" Draco paced the small cell.

Brooke shrugged her shoulders, still trying to catch her breath. "Ain't shit. What the fuck y'all on?"

"You been fuckin wit that work we been bringing in?" Draco stopped pacing the cell and began to walk in circles around her.

"No," Brooke quickly replied.

Rather than smiling in a natural way, Brooke forced it in the mouth instead of the eyes. Her lack of eye contact and wandering eyes gave her away. Not to mention, her body language told a story of deception as well. She began to rub her forehead while still avoiding eye contact. "Why the fuck you lying?" Kalei could see the change in her demeanor instantly.

"Elon made me do it," she blurted out in hopes to save her ass. "I'm sorry. I swear." She raised her hands, and tears began to form in her eyes.

Kalei was in deep thought. With his back against the wall, he put everything into perspective. "Everything making sense now," he whispered. Draco continued to circle Brooke, giving her his famous death stare.

"So, this what's going to happen. It's your responsibility to bring the shit in now," Draco demanded.

"What the fuck?" Brooke whined. "Draco, how? Kalei, why you not sayin' shit?" She looked to Kalei to come to her defense, but he ignored her once more.

"Bitch, you anything," he whispered, waving her off.

"Yale is dead, so now, you have to replace her," Draco stated.

"The fuck you mean she dead?" Brooke asked, frightened.

Kalei sighed, shaking his head. "He means what he said. She in the ground, girl."

"Well," Brooke tried to reason with them, "if I bring them in, what the fuck I'm going do about Elon?"

"Don't let him get that shit," Draco replied sarcastically. "Or that's your ass."

"What the fuck, Moe," Brooke whispered.

"Next assignment." Kalei joked.

"Yeah, next assignment." Draco followed up. "That nigga, Chico, time for him to go."

"Yeah," Kalei interjected. "We need you to pull one of dem ones."

"One of your regulars." Draco joked.

"Fuck y'all," Brooke sassed, rolling her eyes.

"No, fuck you. You got your instructions so get goin," Draco demanded. He gave her some space and showed her to the door.

"Fuck y'all for real," she spat on her way out.

Chapter 7

Isla dragged through the halls of the facility as she made her way to her office. Sluggishly, she crept into her space and threw her belongings where she wanted. With her being a newbie, she had no idea the pressure of the demands the job brought. In all honesty, she wasn't sure if she could comfortably manage. Between the conflict with the staff and higher ups, threats, and security, she wanted to scream. She couldn't figure out why Rita hadn't taken the necessary steps to ensure her employees were not subjected to unnecessary stress. She missed the red flags during the interview process, but now, she was realizing she hated the job. She didn't have any other jobs lined up, and she had no idea what was next for her. What she did know was that she wouldn't be able to keep this one up.

The work environment was more hostile than it should have been. She found it difficult due to the negatives and the manipulation, not to mention the entitlement. The coworkers stressed her the most. They rarely did any work and often created conflict.

Isla instantly grew aggravated by the sudden knock on the door. Before she could acknowledge it, the guard let himself in and delivered his message.

"Warden would like to see you in her office." The guard relayed his message and went on his way. As he shut the door behind him, Isla sighed loudly and damn near strained herself rolling her eyes.

Isla made her way to Rita's office, somewhat on edge. A part of her was nervous, and the other half just didn't give two fucks. Rita had been giving her the side eye since she offered the job, not to mention her witty remarks here and there when it came to the inmates' wellbeing and mental health.

Rita's issue was, of course, with Elon not being able to contain himself. He had googly eyes for Isla, and she took note of it when she came in for the interview. That simply didn't sit well with her, but nevertheless, she thought highly of Isla.

"Good morning, Ms. Harrison, how are you feeling?" Rita greeted her with all smiles and a chipper tone.

Isla was on edge and at the mercy of her imagination as she wondered what Rita could possibly want with her.

Isla took note of the bruising Elon had left her with but

kept her input to herself. "Good morning, Warden. I'm well," she dryly responded. "What about yourself?"

Rita smirked. "That was dry." She slid halfway onto her desk table.

Isla shrugged her shoulders. "It was cordial." She felt a flicker of irritation.

"Understandable. I don't blame your hesitation, but I didn't bring you here to quarrel." She assured.

Isla raised her eyebrow, folding her arms. "Speak your peace, ma'am." She gave her the floor.

"I'd like to gain some clarity on this little love triangle you've got goin on with Devyn and Kalei," Rita pried.

Anger stirred within her, causing her temper to spark. "Excuse me?" Isla rose to her feet. "Ain't no damn love triangle," she shouted. "Devyn is making it more than what it is simply because she wants it to be more than a friendship. That's it. It's that simple." She defended herself.

Rita smirked and nodded. "I'm sure there are others who would say otherwise."

"Well, look, I don't give a fuck what Devyn has to say. I know wassup." Isla's tone was harsh. She spoke through clenched teeth.

"Okay, Ms. Harrison. That was it, just wanted to clear the air," Rita expressed.

Isla turned on her heels and headed for the door.

She allowed the door to slam behind her.

Elon paced the hall corridors repeatedly, back and forth.

He was tense, and it had been evident in his voice. The pitch was higher, and his face was tighter when he spoke, as if he could feel it in his chest. Elon hyper-focused and excessively analyzed the same thoughts daily to the point it had begun to disrupt his day-to-day life. He found it difficult to take action or make any type of decisions, and he could never seem to shake particular thoughts from his mind. His frustration fueled his irrational behavior. Startled, Isla jumped without hesitation as her office door swung open. Elon made his grand entrance while stuck in deep thought.

Isla let her guard down; she could feel the heat brewing inside of her.

Isla's smile instantly turned into a scowl. She clenched her jaws and fist, and rage flowed through her like lava.

Isla sucked her teeth and rolled her eyes as hard as she could. The sight of Elon made her cringe. She had to admit that he put on a good front when they first met, but he took no time showing his true colors. He was a rude, stuck up, entitled prick with a huge jealousy issue.

Elon, on the other hand, had no issue with Isla. In fact, he lowkey wanted to fuck her, but the thought of an inmate being inside her made him wince. All in all, in his mind, Isla was collateral damage. He actually liked her and the initiative she took with the inmates. But that changed when Devyn outed her.

"Can I help you?" Isla sassed with one hand on her hip.

Paying her the slightest bit of attention, he nodded. "I

cleared your schedule for the next thirty minutes," he slurred sarcastically. "Hope you don't mind."

Isla sucked her teeth. "What the fuck? Who the fuck do y'all think y'all are around here?"

"I'm the man in charge! Don't get it fucked up!" Elon rushed to invade Isla's space. He hovered over top of her.

"Look, what you need, Elon?" Isla rolled her eyes, under pressure.

Elon shrugged his shoulders and shook his head. "I need to vent, get some shit up off my chest," he confessed. "And possibly get some advice."

Isla staggered to her seat. Falling into the plush chair, she kicked her feet up and was all ears.

"Advice?" she giggled, asking rhetorically. "We shall see. Wassup?"

Elon leaned back and stretched his arms out. He sighed deeply. "Brother tryin to come for my position."

"How so?" Isla asked.

"He wants what I have. It's obvious," Elon responded.

"Is it? Or do you want what he has?" Isla challenged him. "What is it that you aim for?"

"Money, power, respect, and loyalty," he replied instantly.

"All of which Dean gets?" Isla asked, trying to get to the root.

"I want that power." Elon began to beat on his chest, which was now heaving up and down. "That shit belongs to me, not him!" His voice cracked.

"Entitlement," Isla whispered.

Elon sucked his teeth. "Call it what you want. That nigga gotta go."

Isla raised an eyebrow, tilting her head to the side. "Like dead?"

"Anywhere but here," Elon clarified.

"I think you two need to sit down and talk. Perhaps you all will be able to resolve the issue." Isla tried reasoning with him.

Elon leaned back onto the sofa and folded his arms. "Ain't shit to talk about," he hissed.

"Clearly it is. In my opinion, it looks like it's stemming from jealously," she argued.

"I ain't jealous of that nigga." He flared his nostrils, flexing his jaw muscles.

"Then what would you call it?" Isla rolled her eyes, waiting for his response.

"I said what I said." Elon rose to his feet. "Matter of fact, wassup with you and my brother anyway? You fuckin him too, ain't you?"

Isla grinned and shook her head. "The fuckin audacity," she whispered under her breath.

"Bitch, please. I already know wassup wit you and Kalei." He joked, making his way out.

"You don't know shit. Get the fuck out my office." Isla launched a clipboard filled with papers in his direction, hitting the door, missing him by seconds.

Elon surveyed and scanned the corridors as he observed each inmate carefully. Eyeballing everything in sight, Chico was caught from his peripheral.

"Oh, yeah," Elon whispered. He extended his arm and reached for Chico. He forcefully dragged him, causing him to stumble backwards.

After the slight altercation between Chico and Kalei after his arrival, Elon did his research. Word on the street was that Chico and Kalei had been enemies since teens. Elon figured Chico wouldn't have a problem getting Kalei out the way for the both of them, so he tried his hand.

"The fuck, nigga?" Chico smacked Elon's hands from his shoulders and sized him up.

Elon smirked and nodded his head in approval. "Need you to do me a favor."

"Nigga, I ain't doing shit for you." Chico scoffed and continued walking as he fixed his clothing.

"You look out for me, I look out for you," Elon added, causing Chico to spin around out of curiosity.

"And what's in it for me?" He contemplated with Elon.

"How bout reduced time?" Elon bargained with the inmate.

Chico rolled his eyes, sucking his teeth. "And how the fuck you goin pull that off? Nigga, you ain't no judge. You in corrections."

Elon smirked and shrugged his shoulders. "Corrections with the right connections." Elon jazzed him up, knowing damn well there wouldn't be much he could do for him, especially with the predicament he was about to insert himself in. "Don't be so shallow."

"The fuck is up?" Chico gave in. Inmates were starting to stare, and he didn't like when people started to talk.

"I need you to get Kalei and Draco out my way," he stated. "Need you to wreak a little havoc, get em wild up."

Chico picked with his chin hair and squinted as he thought about what he was being asked. "For what though? Them niggas ain't bout to be on shit. They bout to get released soon."

Elon stepped closer, invading Chico's personal space, which made him feel uneasy. "Just fuckin do it, dammit, and make it messy!" Elon demanded through clenched teeth.

Brooke surveyed the area as she did her rounds around the tiers. She scanned the room, looking for Chico in particular. She knew the sooner she could get him seduced the quicker she'd be out of Kalei and Draco's debt, the last place she wanted to be.

"These niggas want me to bring in drugs; they want me to distract niggas and some more shit. Why me? Huh?" she whispered to herself. "Sick of this damn job."

She took note of an ajar door and sprung in action. Skipping toward the cell, to her surprise, it was assigned to Chico.

BINGO! she thought to herself.

She observed her surroundings once more before she slid inside.

"Fuck is up witchu?" Chico flung the magazine he was reading across the room. He stood to his feet, giving Brooke his undivided attention.

Brooke seductively bit her lip, inching closer to Chico. She whispered in his ear. "I'm on whatever you on." She tugged on his overalls.

Chico smirked, nodding his head. "Oh, yeah, is that right?" He instantly gripped his dick as he bit his bottom lip. His blood pressure and heart rate increased as his penis began to stand up. Engorged and sensitive, he was ready for some action. Brooke gently pushed him backwards as she began the show. Unable to dim the lights, she still managed to work her magic. Slowly, she unbuttoned her blouse, allowing it to hit the floor. She then pushed the straps of her bra to the side, exposing her DD breasts. Lastly, she removed her baton, mace, and belt, causing her uniform pants to drop. Her curvy body and plump, round ass were exactly what Chico had been yearning for.

Brooke placed her hands over Chico's pants and rubbed softly. He sighed as his penis throbbed at the sudden attack. She slid inside and squeezed his balls, and Chico was enjoying every bit of her touch. He wasted no time yanking her from the uniform. He took one breast in his mouth and rolled her nipple with his tongue. She could feel them harden while the other hand caressed her back. He gave her long strokes from the back of her neck to the crack of her ass. Brooke pushed him back, abruptly ceasing him as he fell into the hard, metal bunk. She dropped to her knees and began to tug at the elastic of his briefs. As she brought them down to his thighs, Chico's hungry monster sprang out. The handsome mass of veins made Brooke's eyes light up as it throbbed up and down uncontrollably. She gazed at his pulsating penis, lightly touching it. Chico let out a long gob of precum, a thick string. Brooke rubbed the precum over her breasts and then her mouth. She then gently cupped him and firmly massaged his balls.

"Ohhhhhh," Chico whispered out. He spread his legs wide. Brooke's hands were grazing his thighs as her fingers were stroking his large testes. She went from the top of his penis and then stopped at the frenulum just to rub it.

"Ahhhhhh," he groaned once more but this time from the depth of his stomach as his balls were being taken care of. The frenulum rub was the most gratifying part for a man, and Brooke was well versed at it.

She brought him to her mouth and gave the most exciting flicks of her tongue. Chico's pulsating monster was going crazy. Her wet, salivating tongue gave him rapid lashes like a whip.

His thighs shook uncontrollably as a huge gob of cum erupted, followed by a series of eruptions.

"Let's make this shit quick, bruh." Kalei looked over his shoulder at Draco, who had been preparing himself also. He peeped in and out of the cell, making sure no guards were in sight. Kalei quickly retrieved his homemade shank, tucked it inside his drawers, and gave Draco a head nod. The duo stepped out of the cell, both scanning the pod, making sure everything was in order. Kalei studied the room; he paid attention to the faces and took note of Brooke being MIA.

He grinned slyly, knowing that she had succeeded. It was impossible for a nigga to turn down pussy behind the wall.

"It's down a few more doors, bro," Draco whispered with his eyes both peeled on the inmates and the cell doors.

Draco stopped a few feet away and posted up for the time being. His job was to make sure nobody went in or out until Kalei handled his business, and anyone that interfered had to deal with Draco.

Kalei scanned each cell, peering through the small glass windows. He took a peek into Chico's cell and shook his head. Between Brooke's ass tooted up in the air and Chico lacking, he couldn't figure out which was a better sight. Brooke had him on his back, while she straddled him.

"Ahhhh, fuckkkk," Chico moaned as Brooke bopped up and down on his manhood.

While Chico was stuck in pleasure and ecstasy, Kalei slipped inside the cell undetected, swiftly but without a sound.

He shook his head once more as he tiptoed closer. Chico's eyes had been shut tight, and he was oblivious as to what had been going on.

Brooke whipped her neck in Kalei's direction and knew that was her cue. She quickly hopped off Chico instantly. She staggered around the cell, trying to locate her uniform and dress quickly.

"What the fuckkkk?!" Chico rose from the bed, but his words got caught.

Kalei rushed him, snatching the blade from the left to the right side of his neck, leaving the cleanest cut.

Chico's trachea was instantly severed, preventing him from screaming. Kalei also severed the carotid artery, which prevented new oxygenated blood from reaching his brain. Not to mention, the jugular vein was damaged. All in all, it brought unconsciousness within the blink of an eye, taking thirty seconds or less. Kalei paused as he watched Chico claw at his neck; he took giant gasping breaths through his severed windpipes, gargling blood and coughing.

Kalei completed his mission and went on his way. He quickly scurried out of the cell with Draco right behind him. In unison, they galloped through the tier until they reached their cells. Kalei passed the blade to Draco; he nodded and would dispose of it before they linked back up with each other.

Kalei slid into his cell right before the alarm rang out. He stripped from the bloody clothing and tucked it under his mattress within seconds. Falling back onto the uncomfortable metal bunk, he grabbed a magazine and skimmed through with his feet crossed. He shut his eyes while trying to control his breathing as he waited for the guards to come in and snatch him up. He waited; he knew it was coming.

Once the alarm blared, Elon flashed a sinister grin, knowing that he had won. He knew Kalei wouldn't be able to resist himself and getting his lick back was a must. Elon rounded his warrant unit up, and they made their way to Kalei's cell. Surrounding the door, on count they entered as one hastily. Upon arrival, they weren't expecting Draco to be in the cell with him, but Elon gave them the say so to grab them both. They were both cuffed and dragged to the restricted housing unit. Thrown into a small strip search room, they were demanded to remove their clothing, lift their balls, bend over, and spread their cheeks. Afterwards, they dressed themselves back into jumpsuits and were escorted to the worst block.

"You straight, bruh?" Kalei shouted behind him to Draco.

"Always." Draco flashed a smile and chuckled.

The duo tiptoed down the hall, shackled, until they reached their destination. The noise, the awful smell, and the atmosphere was horrible.

ISLA SAT BEHIND HER DESK, unloading the contents of her stomach into the small waste basket. The sound of the alarm caused her quaking body to jump in an instant. The alarm never meant anything good, so she rushed to the door, scanning the halls. They were now packed with admins and guards scurrying frantically.

Brooke brushed past her unintentionally, and Isla quickly yanked her back, desperately wanting to be in the loop.

"What's goin on?" she asked, concerned.

"We on lockdown. Inmate found dead," she slurred nervously.

Isla sensed the interaction was off, but she maintained her composure and kept her observations to herself.

"What inmate?" she pried.

Brooke dramatically shrugged her shoulders. "Jefferson and Nicks handled that shit," she confessed, shaking her head with a distressed look on her face.

"Kalei!" Isla shouted.

Isla rushed back inside her office to collect belongings while Brooke continued to fill her in.

"It's nothing you can do; he's been sent to solitary," Brooke whispered as she watched Isla rummage through her belongings like a mad woman. "He'll be out in a few weeks or maybe a month."

Isla grabbed her large duffle and headed to the door. She ignored Brooke's comments and pushed past her as she made an exit.

Brooke fell back into the walls and let her head drop. She sighed loudly as she thought about the events that had just taken place that she played a part in.

. . .

Lighthaeaded, Isla managed to trudge her way through halls. She maneuvered through the corridors until she hit the exit.

"Fuck!" she shouted over the blaring alarm as she stumbled to her car. She shoved her bags inside then her body. Starting her car instantly, she wasted no time putting it in drive. She was headed to Dean against her better judgement. But nevertheless, he was the only person who could get Kalei out of this jam. Isla retrieved her phone with shaky hands, and she shot Dean a simple text.

YOUR BROTHER HAS KALEI!

Dean glanced at the text message from Isla. He sighed deeply, running his hands over his face. He was a fixer; he always attempted to rescue others from their own suffering, never stopping to consider the fact that he was robbing those of the experience to suffer and their ability to grow. Often times he intervened while others felt he was meddling. While he felt he was being generous, others took it as invasive and judgmental. Dean had boundaries, but they were poor when it came to Kalei. He always came running when Kalei called, and this would be no different. The only thing he'd be changing from today forward was trusting. He would no longer fix but trust. He would trust that others were able to fix and take responsibility and figure things out without his intervention.

Dean was the most caring and loving person Kalei had in his corner. While he wasn't his biological father, he sure had the heart of one and a special place in Kalei's life. He often pondered on his lifestyle and bringing him into the under-world. Dean was bold, direct, and assertive. He took his traits to the extreme as he came across as dominating. And while he looked from other's perspective, he realized he was a criminal. He did destroy societies by pumping them with illegal drugs. He created addicts that had become so dependent on the drugs that they committed crimes to feed their habit. Majority of the crime had been related to Dean, all because he wanted to get some cash without doing too much work. In a single world, in Dean's world, his profession was exhilarating, and the rewards were immense when you were at the top of the food chain.

Tucked away, approximately forty-five-minuets from civi-lization, sat Frankie's mini mansion. The six-bedroom, five-bathroom, three story house sat on two acres of land nestled in the woods of Brandywine. Dean crept up the dirt road with his foot lightly on the gas.

Dean swung the door open and made himself at home. Leaving his shoes at the door, he traveled from the foyer to her cozy entertainment room. Falling into the plush, leather sectional, he kicked his feet up and sighed heavily.

Frankie rocked a short boy cut. She often tried to keep the jet-black look, but the protruding grays wouldn't let her be great. Frankie was slim and petite with a coffee-colored skin complexion. She mirrored majority of Ethiopian women with her looks. Her eyes were beady, round, and a dark shade of brown. Her bottom lip was slightly bigger than her top, and the permanent line that centered in between her chin caused a split. Frankie was caught red handed, pouring both her and Dean a tall glass of Moet. It was her go to when it was time for her to unwind or talk business.

Grabbing each glass, she sauntered across the room and passed Dean his glass. He had made himself comfortable as he stretched out on her leather sectional. Frankie found a spot next to him and nestled in quickly.

"Talk to me." She spoke in a soft tone.

Frankie was Dean's bottom bitch. Frankie had been around for years, long before Dean had ever thought about making Rita his girl. Frankie was everything Dean wanted in a woman - smart, sassy, ruthless, loyal, genuine. The list went on. The only thing that got in their way was business, and it stayed in their way. Frankie couldn't seem to mix her business with her pleasure, and Dean wasn't one to wait around. Frankie wanted Dean in the worst way, but the unknowing scared her.

Dean sighed as he threw back his glass, taking a huge gulp. "I can't wait for the lil nigga to get out. The sooner the better. Before I have to kill my fuckin brother," he stated.

"Still giving you a hard time?" Frankie asked, knowing the answer.

"Is he?" Dean replied dramatically. "He just fuckin with me for the fun of it. He jealous, and I got bigger shit on my plate to deal with than some fuckin sibling rivalry."

Frankie titled her cup, taking a sip. "I agree." She nodded her head.

"This shit frustrating, man." Dean shook his head, throwing his glass back once again.

Frankie was the woman in charge on the east coast. She was the supplier and the distributor; all in all, she was the connect. She was Dean's boss, and he answered to her.

"How about we handle this in the morning?" Frankie stood to her feet and snatched the empty glass from his grasp. She sat the glasses down and returned, exposing her naked body. "And in the meantime, you just relax."

Frankie wanted Dean, and she was going to have him, no matter what it took. She moved in, tenderly pecking him before his tongue penetrated her lips. Their tongues danced as he noticed she had nothing on. He caressed her soft breasts and began nuzzling and licking them gently as her body gyrated in response. Frankie stroked his thick manhood, and they explored one another. Dean moved one hand between her legs and began rubbing her wet pussy. At first, she backed away, but in an instant, she gave in, allowing his finger to slip inside her. Frankie grinded on his hand as he slipped a second finger in, and she pumped harder and faster.

Suddenly, Dean rose to his feet and placed them in a sixty-nine position. Frankie knew the drill. She got on top of Dean and straddled his face as she leaned over and dropped her head in his lap. His tongue brushed over her pulsating bosom, and she cried out. She took the head of his dick in her mouth and sucked slowly. Dean moaned as he stuffed his tongue inside of her vagina, and she bobbed her head up and down. He wrapped his hands around her small ass, pulling her against his face as he tongue fucked her. Frankie rubbed his balls, deep throating him.

She pulled away and sat up, indicating she was ready to move to another position. Dean lifted her from his face and casually rolled her onto her back. He positioned himself between her legs as he took his time sliding his rod inside of her. Tears filled Frankie's eyes. She blinked, and the tears fell as Dean shoved the entire length of his rock-hard penis inside of her in one fast thrust. They moaned in unison as he began to thrust her with tender strokes. She pulled him closer to her, and Dean kissed her neck, causing her nipples to harden, and her cheeks flushed with excitement.

More tears fell from her eyes as he started pounding away harder and faster. Frankie knew he was going to cum at any moment, and she so badly wanted his hot, gooey load inside of her. She slammed her hips against his body, taking him deep inside of her as her juices flooded his manhood.

"Fuckkkkkk!" She moaned as her orgasm came and went while Dean continued ramming into her, nearing his breaking point.

"Damnnnnnn," he grunted, tightening his grip on her hips just as he unleashed his load inside of her in several short spurts.

The room was silent, but Dean remained where he was. He eyeballed Frankie with a lustful smile as the beads of sweat dripped from his body onto her breasts.

KANNIN PULLED into the empty gas station and stopped at the pump next to Ty. He leaned back in his seat and watched him carefully through the tinted windows. He had been following him for the past forty-eight hours and decided he had had enough. Ty staggered inside, lacking. He was alone, and from the looks of it, Kannin could tell he wasn't carrying.

Anger and hatred toward Ty were his motivation for revenge. Kannin wanted to enact revenge because it granted him gratification, the feeling of taking back power. He had an instinctive desire to get even. While the victim was behind bars, he was still motivated to attack. Kannin felt as though getting an eye for an eye would bring him closure.

Ty pushed the door open and galloped out cheerfully, as if he had no care in the world. He popped his gas tank open and began pumping. Kannin eased out from his vehicle, removed his pistol he had tucked, and tossed it in his hands. Making his presence known, he slid to the side, so Ty could catch the view.

"Lil nigga, you scared the shit out me." Ty gripped his chest and jumped, now face to face with Kannin and his sinister glare.

"Why you snitch on my brother? What was your reason?" Kannin asked, hoping to get an honest response back.

Ty sucked his teeth and sighed. "Man, don't be walkin' up on me, confronting me bout no shit like that." He got defensive. "Fuck your brother and fuck you too, lil nigga. Don't nobody got time for that shit." Ty grew cockier and more confident by the moment.

Kannin smirked and shook his head. "You do know what happens to snitches, right?" He asked a rhetorical question, not wanting an answer back.

He took note of the huge lump that had formed in Ty's throat, as well as the beads of sweat that congregated on the tip of his nose. He blinked repeatedly as images of his short-lived life flashed before his eyes.

"Since you couldn't give me a decent enough answer, you know what that means." Kannin winked.

Wanting to shut him up for good, Kannin leveled the revolver at Ty's chest. His fingers began to quake as he felt the cold metal grow increasingly heavy as the seconds passed.

"Don't do this." Ty spoke in a soft tone as he pleaded.

Kannin's face grew grimmer. His grip tightened as his finger twitched on the trigger as he pulled it. He watched Ty stumble in place as he stared at the blood in amazement. The shot echoed deafeningly, and his ears started to ring. Ty gripped his chest as he winced right before collapsing to the ground. Kannin stood over top of him and watched his blood ooze into a huge pool. There was a sense of immediate and terrible loss, but it was quickly followed by complete denial and justification. Each decision had surfaced in his mental, reaching his subconscious, until his adrenaline died down.

Kannin felt as if a weight had been lifted from his shoulders after pulling the trigger.

"GREAT, they pulled me out of fuckin bed for a gas station shooting." Reed sighed heavily and shook his head. He took his time, cautiously pulling on a side street. The flashing blue and red lights added to his slight migraine. Bystanders scattered throughout the streets behind the yellow tape while officers on the scene did their best keeping them out.

Reed took a few deep breaths, said a mini prayer, and exited his vehicle. He smoothed over his dingy tee shirt that he usually slept in and stuck his hands in his baggy jean pockets. Lowering his head, he sighed once more when he realized he had stepped out in his house shoes. "Fuckkkk!" He cursed himself but continued.

He pushed past the crowd and stepped over the tape as if he didn't have a care in the world. "What the fuck is this?" he shouted to the forensic examiner on the scene. "You pulled me out of bed for this shit?" Reed spun around dramatically in a circle and then stuck his foot out as if he were striking a pose.

Jake cleared his throat loud enough for Reed to hear him, and he turned on his heels quickly. "You're here because your CI got clipped," he sassed.

Reed instantly turned his tone down and brushed the attitude off. "What CI?"

Jake smirked and shrugged his shoulders. "Lil nigga you got to set up Dean."

Sadness, fear, and anger all hit him at once. It was as if a hot knife had been plunged into his solar plexus. He slowly staggered to the body and lifted the sheet.

Nice and clean, I guess, he thought to himself as he examined the clean hole that set in the middle of Ty's forehead.

While on the hunt for Dean, Reed came across Ty more than often. Kalei was a bit of a hassle, but Ty managed to always be one step behind. When Reed came to the conclusion that he wouldn't be able to get Dean, Kalei was his next victim. But even Kalei seemed to be hard to catch. So, Reed used Ty because he was gullible and all for himself. Ty was able to give Kalei up, and in return, Reed looked the other way. Ty gave Reed everything he needed and more to get Kalei out the game. However, he never thought it would catch back up to him.

Chapter 8

Under the prison's first floor, Kalei was locked in, hearing the echo of everybody who was in a cell with no bars on the doors and nothing in it. There was nothing to read, nothing to do at all besides talk to yourself and think. The seven by nine cement room had a steel door with a slot for receiving meals and a small window to see outside. Inside, there was nothing besides a toilet. Prisoners were only allowed to shower once a week and spend one hour outside each day. It was simply another level of hell for Kalei. It was here that men were made and broken at the same time. The desolateness and the feeling of utter aloneness didn't go unnoticed. Life in the hole was epitomized by one big question mark; uncertainty was always the order of the day.

Kalei's mind began to wonder and wonder. He started

counting the walls and ceiling tiles. He paced heel to toe in a line like a sobriety test for hours. He thanked Allah for a strong mind because, with the way the inmates were acting out, he would have lost his shit a long time ago. One guy banged on his cell door for hours, another inmate threw shit from his opening like a monkey, and two other inmates were slinging it back and forth to one another. While that had been transpiring, Kalei focused on the opportunistic racist across from him. Kalei had never been called out of his name except in the hole. He listened carefully as the inmate began his daily racial slur rant before he asked him.

"Ayeeee, Moe, why the fuck you in here?" Kalei questioned him, so badly wanting to know the answer.

He was mid conversation about how he hated Blacks but stopped to answer Kalei over top of the commotion.

"Because I had a Black cellmate," he shouted. Kalei shook his head, instantly assuming it was a fight, before the inmate finished his sentence. "And I got caught suckin his dick!"

"The fuck?!" Kalei turned his nose up and backed away from the cell door as he listened to the entire block erupt into laughter. He shook his head in disgust, simply because he never knew what weirdos he'd be stuck with. A few months back, they escorted him to a cell where an inmate had already been assigned, but he happened to be waiting. The doors opened, and he was bent over, holding his ass cheeks apart, screaming, "Come on in." Kalei tussled with the guards before they gave him his own cell.

Staying awake through the night in the hole took a toll on Kalei's physical health. Fatigue and low energy had him in a slump. But that was neither here nor there. Kalei had been counting down the days for the last month, and while he was confined, he knew he would make it out somehow. Today was the day he would be released, and nothing or no one was stopping that. He was excited and nervous, but he also wondered if anything from his past would come back to bite him. Nevertheless, he was ecstatic about getting out, even though fear plagued him. He didn't know what to expect on the other side of the fence, but he was ready.

He scooted to the opposite wall and placed his back against it.

"It's about that time, bruh," Kalei shouted, hoping Draco would hear him well enough, and he did.

"I know, and if I ain't already told you, I'm proud of you, brotha!" Draco replied.

"Naw, I'm proud of us!" Kalei corrected him as he thought about their time in together, all of the obstacles and challenges they went through to get to this day.

"You better go hard when you get out there, nigga!" Draco chastised. "Do everything the right way! Keep your head on a swivel and don't let nobody get one up on you! I mean that!" Draco coached him through the thick concrete wall.

Kalei smirked and replied. "Or what?" He joked.

"Or that's your ass!" Draco laughed, but he was muffled

due to the sounds from the other inmates that were locked away. "For real, man, I don't wanna see you back in here."

"I promise not to come back, bro." Kalei assured him.

"I love you, nigga," Draco whispered but loud enough to reach Kalei.

He nodded and allowed a tear to drop. "I love you more, brodie."

Dean sighed deeply as he entered the facility with Frankie on his heels. She had demanded she tag along and have a pep talk with Rita herself. Dean played a major role in how smoothly Frankie's operation ran behind the wall, but that was with the help of Rita. Not to mention, Elon's jealousy got in the way. Frankie staggered slowly behind Dean, allowing her heels to echo throughout the halls, and they hit the pavement melodically.

"This her officer right here," Dean whispered under his breath with slight hesitation.

Frankie grinned slyly. Gently, she shoved him to the side and shot him a piercing stare. "You'll know when we done," she stated.

Frankie turned her back, and swinging the door open, she quickly shut it once inside.

Rita sat in her desk chair with her feet kicked up and head resting while her eyes were shut tight. Frankie shook her head as she inched into the office space. She studied the area and turned her nose up at the furnishings and decor.

"Mmm, but that's expected," she whispered to herself

before clearing her throat.

Rita jumped up from the weak slumber, gasping for air.

"Long time no see." Frankie grinned. She eased on top of the desk and crossed her legs.

Frankie smirked, and Rita's heart skipped a beat when she saw Frankie's face. It had been years since their last encounter, and Frankie was the last person she wanted to see. Rita despised Frankie, and it was all over Dean. After being trapped in multiple love quarrels with Elon, Rita attempted to double back, but things didn't go as planned. Frankie had always been around, but Rita knew her to be the one in charge. It wasn't until they grew closer that Rita realized she had lost. While they never made their relations public, Rita knew what the deal was between them, and that hurt her to the core. Frankie, on the other hand, boasted about Dean every chance she could get. It was in her nature to get under Rita's skin, and it was simply because she knew she'd never step out of line, and if she did, it would be her pleasure handling her. Rita, at a loss for words, thought her mind had been playing tricks on her. "Uhhh," she mumbled.

"It's me in the flesh." Frankie joked. "It's a shame I have to come back around on these terms, but your husband has been fuckin up my money, and that is not okay." Frankie stared blankly in the air.

Rita rolled her eyes and dropped her head, allowing it to hit the desk, causing a loud thump.

"I'll handle it." She spoke under her breath.

"Oh, I know you will. I'm sure you'll take the necessary precautions as well to ensure this doesn't happen again," Frankie sassed. "My money, my money, Rita. You better tell your man."

"I said I'll handle it." Rita popped up from her seat, invading Frankie's space. She sat, unfazed, and smirked. "You can go now." Rita raised her voice.

Frankie laughed dramatically. "Oh, you do not have to tell me twice. I just came to give you a warning or what I like to call pep talk." She slid off the table and headed toward the door. "I don't feel you need a warning; you already know wassup."

Frankie spoke her peace and swung the door open wildly, letting herself out. Rita stood, planted in place, with her arms folded.

Rita speed walked through the halls of the facility until she reached the east wing.

"Ughhhhhhh!" She shouted as she pushed past inmates and moved around guards.

Galloping down the hall, she burst through Isla's office door. With no greeting, she instead slammed the door shut and began to pace the room as if she were alone.

Twice in one week, Isla thought to herself as she remembered Elon doing the exact same thing the day prior.

Isla stared at Rita in amazement as she had never seen her act so irate. She smirked a bit seeing her lose her shit.

"Can I help you with something, Warden?" Isla asked her,

looking the least bit interested in her problems.

"I'm losing my shit, Ms. Harrison." She paced the small office space, running her fingers through her hair. "This job, my past lifestyle, my husband that can't keep his dick in his pants or his hands to himself, my ex who happens to be his brother, these inmates, the drugs, the money, the politics. "Arghhhh!" She shouted with frustration.

Isla stared blankly at Rita, batting her eyelashes. "That's a lot," she mumbled.

With her chest heaving up and down, slightly on the verge of tears, she took deep breaths.

She began. "I betrayed the man I loved for his brother. I wish I could take it all back." A tear slid from one eye. "Elon is nothing like Dean, and I hate myself every day for the decision I made." She wiped the snot from her nose on her blouse. "Now, he got this bitch coming in my place of work, trying to undermine me."

Isla nodded her head and just listened. She didn't cut her off nor did she interrupt her. She allowed Rita to release all of what sounded like pent up emotions.

"What's crazy is that it seems like the inmate I'm fuckin is the only cure to all my problems. He makes everything go away," she confessed. "Then, it all comes back. My life is in shambles, and I don't know what to do. I don't even know where to start to identify the problem at hand." She began to sob silently, wiping her tears away as they came.

Isla cleared her throat before she began. "I think you need

to relax, Warden." She reached out and gently grabbed Rita's hand. "I also think you may need to take some time off. For you. For your mental. Get you straight. Bring yourself back because, clearly, this isn't you," Isla preached. "As far as Dean, what's for you will always be for you, and it won't ever miss you. That is what I know to be factual. Everything is aligned as it should be. Everything is happening the way it should." Isla's words soothed Rita. "Obviously, you two weren't meant to be as bad as you feel you were. And as far as Elon and Draco go..." Isla began but was cut off mid-sentence.

Rita shrieked and turned pale as if it were a secret still.

"I don't even know what to say about that, and yes, I know, but your secret is safe with me." Isla assured her. "I honestly think you need to heal, not for them but for you."

The two women sat in silence for several seconds. Isla held her hand and allowed her to be vulnerable in this moment. Rita's silent sobs filled the room.

"Kalei is scheduled to be released in a few hours," Rita managed to mumble.

Isla nodded and dropped her head. "I'm well aware. What's really unfortunate is that your husband had him thrown into confinement." She rolled her eyes.

Rita agreed. "What's unfortunate is the fact that he set the entire thing up. Now, I have a dead inmate on my hands, and the one responsible is soon to be released."

Isla shook her head in disgust. "Elon is a..."

"Cancer, such a horrible person. I have no idea who or what made him this way, but I want no parts. This is it!" Rita stood to her feet, straightening her pant suit out. "This is where I put my foot down and stand my ground."

Isla smirked as she scanned Rita over, taking note of the newfound confidence.

"I'm going to let Kalei out, so he can get ready to be discharged," Rita stated with sincerity in her eyes. "Thank you, Isla, for listening."

Isla, with watery eyes, nodded her head and whispered back. "No, thank you." Her voice cracked. Rita headed for the door and shut it behind her, leaving Isla stuck with her thoughts.

Rita maneuvered through the corridors and descended six flights of steps until she reached the isolation unit. After nodding her head, a guard posted near the entrance led her down the hall. Rita winced and turned her nose up at the smell, the eerie silence, and the rundown condition the prison had been in this particular area of the prison.

She eyeballed the cell doors and pointed at Kalei and Draco's cells.

"I need them out… NOW!" she shouted with a smug expression. Turning on her heels, she made her way back up the flights of steps before she released a breath and inhaled the fresh air.

Jesus Christ, she thought to herself as flashes of the isolation wing flickered through her brain.

Chapter 9

After he was taken from the hole, they directed him to the showers. Kalei stepped into the gym like setting where the paint had peeled off the walls; he grinned hard as this would be his last time here. The shower heads leaked onto the rusted concrete floor. The floors were disgustingly slimy, but he had shower shoes for that very reason. Little water ran out, but it was enough for Kalei to freshen up. Lathering up, he rinsed off quickly. He was given five minutes, and that was all he needed. Staying awake through the night was taking a toll on his health, but there was no choice in the hole. Today was the day he would be free. He was excited and nervous, and he wondered if there was anything from his past that might come up. He felt his heart beating rapidly, as if it were to burst out of his chest. He was afraid to leave Draco behind, not knowing his outcome, but there was a bit of relief. Kalei was called to receiving and discharge and given his clothes, wallet, and other belongings. Correctional officers asked him a series of questions to verify his identity and allowed him to sign papers. He was then escorted to the front of the prison. Unlike most inmates, he refused a halfway house. Walking out the door, he was met by Isla.

Devyn sat in her car, ducked below the seat but was just high enough so that she could peep through the window. She glanced at Isla waiting on Kalei to be released.

Wild bitch, she thought to herself as her expression turned smug.

Devyn was filled with bitterness and resentment; she had been angry for days. She felt wronged in so many ways, as if she had gotten the shorter end of the stick. While Isla didn't lead her on, she still blamed her for her unhappiness. Unable to forgive, she decided to carry the hate. And here she was, ready to take out her anger. The headaches, the heartaches, it had all escalated to this very moment.

She hated Isla for not loving her back, but now, she hated her even more. Not only did she not love her back, but she was in love with Kalei, which had been apparent.

Devyn wanted revenge. She wanted to make Isla hurt, and by doing that, she planned on killing two birds with one stone. She figured once she eliminated Kalei, Isla would have no other choice but to come running back to her. Plus, while Ty's murderer was still on the loose, she knew Kalei was the one responsible, so him going was the icing on the cake. Regardless of him being a snitch or not, he was blood, he was family, and she was going to make that known.

Isla stood outside the gates, waiting patiently. Her heart was warm and filled with joy, but the not knowing who the father of her child was also lingering. She wished she could rewind the hands of time, but she knew it wasn't possible, so she decided to take the secret to the grave with her. She prayed the baby belonged to Kalei and not his little brother.

Kalei staggered out the front door and dragged his way through the gates. Isla waited for him eagerly, and she jumped into his arms as soon as he crossed the threshold. He squeezed her tight, not wanting to let go. With bags in one hand and Isla occupying the other, he forced his bottoms back onto his waist and continued to squeeze her with all his might.

Isla roughly grabbed his head, and rotating it from side to side, she planted kisses all over.

"Best day of my life," she whispered, draping her arm across his shoulder.

Devyn swung her door open, aimed her gun at Kalei, and pulled the trigger without hesitation. The shot echoed deafeningly, and she watched as the bullet punched its way through Kalei's neck, causing a gaping hole that instantly squirted blood.

The unexpected bullet that punched through Kalei's chest sent an electrifying jolt through Isla's body, leaving her speechless. A soul-deep shiver of disbelief coursed through her veins, leaving her in a daze.

Kalei hit the ground, and Isla went right down with him. Wrapping her arms around him, she squeezed his wound tight and applied as much pressure as she could.

Kalei's eyes barely registered the flicker of light before the sound struck him like a slap. He didn't feel pain or impact; instead, he felt massive heat that eventually turned into throbbing numbness. He knew something had happened, but his mind hadn't caught up with it.

"Kalei, baby, listen to me." Isla sobbed. "Do not fuckin leave me! Do you hear me?!" she shouted. "We just started over. You can't go."

Kalei, unable to speak, blinked repeatedly, letting Isla know he was still responsive. He gripped her body and held her tightly.

Devyn stood back and watched the scene. Her sly grin immediately turned into a mild cry as she hit the ground, beating it with her bare hands.

THE HEART MONITOR BEEPED STEADILY. Isla batted her lashes, forcing her eyes open. The pungent smell of hospital disinfectant invaded her nostrils. The room had been silent with the exception of her heavy breathing and the sounds indicating she was still alive. Isla opened one eye after the other, squinting to sharpen the images before her. She glanced around, taking in the deserted blue and white color schemed bedroom.

"What the fuck? I thought Kalei got shot, not me. What am I laid up in here for?" Several thoughts coursed through her mind.

"Welcome back." Kalei greeted her. After his surgery, he insisted on sitting by Isla's bedside until she woke from her deep slumber one bullet, seven stitches, and thirteen hours later.

"Kalei!" Isla's wide eyes began to water.

"Shhhhhhhh," Kalei whispered. He grabbed her hand and squeezed it tightly. "You need to relax, for the both of you."

Still a bit groggy, Isla smirked. "I'm glad you're okay." She flashed a pearly white smile back at him.

"I'm glad my girls are too," he replied.

Very weak, Isla still managed to release the laughter inside. "What girls are you talking about, silly?" She questioned him, assuming he had been referring to her twins that sat on her chest, but she was wrong.

"You and the one you're carrying."

Isla gasped loudly with wild eyes.

THE END

Did you enjoy the read?

Let us know how much by leaving us a review on Amazon
and Goodreads.

Keep reading for a preview of…

A Set Up For Revenge

By Ashley Williams

CHAPTER 1

My name was Cameron, but everyone called me Babygirl. From my mother's womb until I was about eight years old, I'd always lived in small places. Due to my father's lifestyle, I'd been in and out of hotels all throughout the states. My father, Jonathan, was a pimp and a drug dealer. Before she was murdered, my mother, Wanda, was an addict but wanted to beat the addiction to crack so bad. At least she acted like it.

Along with being an addict, my mother was very evil. She let my father beat me and even tried selling me to his clients without a care in the world. I can't count how many times I'd ran away, wondering why my mother would do this to me. A mother was supposed to love and nurture her child, and with me being a young girl, one would think that would be my mother's sole purpose. Unfortunately, it wasn't.

Things only went from bad to worse as the years went by and as I grew older. Life became harder, and eventually, tragedy struck. My mother was *unintentionally* killed by my father. He had shot at an intruder who made his way inside our small home, and my mother was caught in the crossfire as she moved about our dark house to safety. She was shot in her chest and died instantly.

My father was arrested that night but was subsequently acquitted of murder charges after all twelve jurors found him not guilty. If you ask me, he should have gone to jail. The murder may have been an accident, but had my father not been involved with shady people who later became enemies, then maybe my mother would still be alive today. She may have done some dirty things and hurt me in ways no child should ever have to endure, but I still loved her. I thought about her often and found myself envisioning what life would have been like had she loved me just a little bit more.

Alice, one of my father's prostitutes, had been a part of my life for quite some time now and I just loved her. My father had been cheating on my mother with Alice for a while and I knew all about it. As a daughter, my loyalty should've been with my mother and I could've told her about my father and Alice, but with the way she treated me, I really didn't care. Regardless of her dealings with my father behind my mother's back, Alice had always loved and protected me. She never condoned my father mistreating me.

She was more of a mother to me than my biological mother ever was, and I gave her more respect than I could remember giving to my mother. Alice made me feel *seen* and *heard*. She made me feel like I was *special* to her. When my mother died, it made sense for Alice to take on the role as stepmother. A role that she embraced.

I sat in my window on a late, summer night watching the streets, and all I could seem to focus on was my stepmother. I watched her get in and out of cars with strangers, collect money, and stuff it in her bra. At fifteen, I knew what she was doing was wrong, but I would never condemn her in my mind or out loud. The hopping in and out of cars lasted a few hours and I kept watch like her bodyguard in the distance. Not long after she had walked into the house, I could hear my father yelling at her.

"Where is my money hoe? Why is it short?!" His voice echoed through the walls. Alice matched his tone, screaming and hollering, making the situation worse. When I came out of my room my father was dragging Alice through the hallways. I watched as his open hand and closed fist connected with her face. He brutally assaulted her and ripped her clothes from her body. "Bitch, I knew you had my money!" He yelled as he continued his assault with a backhand across her cheek.

Alice always found ways to steal money in order to make sure that I not only had food on the table, but clothes on my back. She knew what she was risking by playing with my father's money, but she did it anyway. After making sure she handed over all of the night's take that she'd worked hard for, my father sent her to her room like she was a child. Satisfied, he left the house, and I immediately ran towards Alice's room. I swung the door open and flew into the room to be by her side. It hurt me to see her hurt.

"Are you okay?"

"Babygirl, I'm okay. You know I'll do anything to take care of and protect you," she proclaimed while holding my hand and looking into my eyes. I felt what she had said was true indeed. I'd always wondered why my stepmother protected me and loved me the way she did when I wasn't really her child. I planned to ask her one day when the time was right.

"Can I get you anything?"

"No Babygirl, just go to your room until I can figure everything out," she replied. I didn't know what she meant by that. I wanted so badly to stay with her in fear that my father would come back for round two, instead I did what I was told.

When he did return back to the house, I could tell that he was both high and drunk. He stood at the entryway of my room and told me he needed to talk to me. I stared up at him with disdain written all over my face as he spoke.

"Babygirl, what Alice did was out of line and I'm sorry you had to witness that. She's been stealing from me, and I finally caught her," he explained. I really wasn't trying to hear it. I knew what she did and didn't care because he deserved it.

I sat on the bed and listened to him talk about nothing for a while, making up excuses as to why he needed to teach Alice a lesson, until she walked in. Her eyes were black, her lips busted and bloody.

My father looked over his shoulders and scolded her. "Get the fuck out, you fat bitch!" Him saying that to her broke my heart because I knew he was only being mean and hateful. Alice looked at my father with tear filled eyes and walked away from the door feeling embarrassed, I'm sure. I looked at him with disgust and shook my head. "You get you some rest and I'll see you in the morning." With that, he left my room, and I laid my head on my pillow with thoughts of me and my stepmother getting away from him.

In the middle of the night, they were right back at it, but this time I didn't hear my father beating on Alice. I guess he figured she'd had enough. I could hear their heated argument through my halfway opened door. My father threw insult after insult at Alice, and I didn't know how she had the strength to sit there and take it.

"Why did you marry me if you didn't accept me as I was, big and all?" I could hear her ask my father.

"I'm still trying to figure that out myself. I'm tired of fussing with you though. If you know like I know, you'll drop this and take yo' ass to bed. I'm still not over the fact that you've been stealing from me and I'm a few minutes off your ass." I only hoped that Alice took heed to what he said and left well enough alone. When I heard no response and saw my father walk past my room towards the back of the apartment, I knew she had.

Relieved, I laid back down and closed my eyes. Before I could get back to sleep, Alice rushed into my room. Her eyes darted around before landing on me. "Pack some of your things, we're leaving." I looked at her and smiled and then looked to my ceiling thanking God for answering my prayers.

Knowing we didn't have much time, I hopped out of bed and scrambled to grab as much of my belongings as I could. Once I was done, she motioned for me to follow her. We ran out of the door as quickly and quietly as possible. Throwing all of our stuff in the backseat of the car, we jumped in and sped off. Never looking back, we left both my father and Louisiana.

We found ourselves in Alice's hometown of Texas, where we moved from hotel to hotel, which was something I was used to. Even if I wasn't used to it, I didn't mind adapting. I was willing to do anything to stay away from my father. Being with Alice, I felt free, and I loved the thought of not having to worry about my father's verbal and physical abuse anymore. That feeling of being free ended all too soon.

One night while I was laying on the bed reading a book, I heard a loud noise. It was so loud, I knew it had to be right outside of our room. I got up from the bed and made my way to the window to see what was going on. My eyes widened when they landed on my father. I watched as he beat on a car window until it shattered. My heart rate sped up when I saw him reach inside the car and pull Alice out. He was yelling so loud, I could hear him all the way in the room.

"Bitch, you thought you could run to Texas, and I wouldn't find you?! You're on my turf and I have people all over this state. Where is Babygirl?!" He barked. Alice didn't utter a peep of my whereabouts.

This only infuriated him, causing him to rain down heavy blows on her body. People went about their business as if the scene was a normal occurrence. Scared, I ran and hid in the closet. From the closet, I noticed the hotel door was slightly open. I had planted myself in the closet, frozen in fear. There was no way I could close it and risk being seen by my father.

I was slender in build, so it was easy for me to curl up on the closet floor to hide myself from his sight. The floor in the closet was filthy, but the thought of having to face him made me fight through it. My mind was racing, and I had that terrible feeling in the pit of my stomach. I never wanted to feel this way again; at least not this soon. Memories of the night my mother was killed flooded my mind.

What if he killed Alice too? I thought to myself. I couldn't lose her. My thoughts were immediately cut short when I heard him bust into our hotel room. I could hear things being tossed around and concluded that he was trashing the place. It didn't sound like he was looking for me, in fact, he never even called out my name. He had to have been looking for whatever money he thought Alice had and drugs.

I had contorted my body in such a way that when he opened the closet door, he didn't notice me amongst the clothing that hung inside. I silently thanked God because if he had looked down, he would've seen me. Finding nothing, he left. When I heard him slam the front door, I let out a sigh of relief and waited for about five minutes before exiting the closet. Pushing the door open slowly, I picked up on how eerily quiet the room was. All of our belongings were thrown about the room and the mattress was turned over.

Rushing to the window in hopes of finding Alice outside, I panicked when I was unable to locate her. Fishing for my cell phone through the mess my father had made, I went to dial her number and paused. Alice had always taught me to think before I set my mind out to do anything. I knew that if she wasn't here then my dad had taken her and calling would be bad for the both of us. Here I was, a young girl, with no place to go, leftovers in the microwave, a few dirty clothes to put on, and no money.

I thought things like this only happened in movies, but reality had set in really quick that it was happening to me, and I had to accept it. I never knew my grandparents and I highly doubted any of my aunts would want me, so I opted to not call any of them. I was strong for the most part and Alice had taught me how to survive as best she could. I decided that I would wait to see how things played out. Taking my time to put the room back together, I listened to the radio for a while and wondered how many nights Alice had paid to stay in the room. I jumped up after the thought and rushed to the lobby. In such a rush, I almost fell walking in and the man sitting at the front desk giggled a little before asking me if I was okay.

"Yes, I'm fine," I replied, embarrassed. "I'm in room 212, and I need to know how many nights I have left to stay here before I have to pay again?"

"You should know that," he retorted. I ignored his smart comment. I wasn't in the position to go back and forth with this man, so I just waited for his answer. Looking down at the computer, he clicked a few buttons and looked back up at me. "It's paid for eleven more days." I sighed and thanked him, then turned to walk away. "If you need more time, I'm sure we can work something out, if you know what I mean." I heard him say from behind me.

I knew exactly what he meant and when I turned around and saw his creepy eyes staring at me with a mouthful of tobacco, I quickly made my exit. Back in my hotel room, I ran myself a bath to wash off the dirt from the closet as well as the old man's dirty stare. After taking an hour-long bath, I began to think of my next move. In the corner of the room, I eyed Alice's make-up bag, clothes, and Ziploc bag full of condoms. I knew I couldn't fit her clothes, but everything else was a go.

I was still a virgin, but I felt like it couldn't be that hard to use what I had to get what I wanted. Alice had sex for money every night and nothing happened to her. She returned home each night, with tired eyes but for the most part, she seemed alright. I mean, she was right back to it the next night like clockwork. I stood in the mirror, admiring my body, and the thought faded into my imagination. *"No way,"* I thought to myself. *"There has to be another way."*

The next night as my stomach growled, thoughts of working the streets came back to my mind. With no money and no alternative, I got dressed in heels and the only dress that I packed. I put on red lipstick, put my hair in a high pony-tail, and applied mascara and eyeliner just as I'd seen Alice do plenty of times. To look at the finished work, I grabbed the mirror that was left behind. I was amazed at how different and grown I looked.

Here it was a Thursday night, and I was about to do something I would probably regret later. I took one last glimpse at my innocent face and headed out the door. I didn't know the first place to begin so I turned and walked towards the lobby. The thought of that man at the front desk gave me the shivers, but I kept walking in that direction. Surprisingly when I stepped inside of the lobby, it was a woman standing behind the desk and not the pervert.

"May I help you?" The lady asked with a friendly smile. Looking down at my attire, I put my head down, ashamed, and walked out of the hotel without responding. Stepping outside, I was startled by a tall guy with tattoos that painted his neck. I admired his long beard and muscular frame. Figuring he could be my potential first customer, I shot him a seductive look as if I knew what I was doing.

"How old are you?" He asked.

"Eighteen," I lied. He asked me to get into his car and although hesitant, I followed as he walked in front of me. In my mind I was thinking, *wow this is really about to go down.* Sitting in the passenger seat, I avoided eye contact with him and went for what I knew and started to touch myself sexually. I leaned over and touched his face, still in disbelief that I was doing such things. I went to reach for the big bulge in between his legs, but he did something unexpectedly; he grabbed my hand.

"Why are you out here doing these things?"

Annoyed, I leaned back in my seat with an attitude. "Look, I'm just out here trying to make some money."

"Why?" He questioned further.

"Because I have to pay for my hotel room and buy food. Is there anything wrong with that, mista?" I clapped my hands at him. He pulled out a few hundreds and handed them to me. "What's the catch? And how can I repay you?" I asked with my eyes big in amazement.

"Just stay out of these streets, that's the catch. Next time, you won't be so lucky and run into somebody like me. You will get what you're looking for from one of these thugs out here." I slowly got out of the vehicle, embarrassed yet again.

How can I be so stupid? This had always worked for Alice, but I wasn't her. Heading back into the hotel, I made me way to my room. I wanted so bad to grab the phone and call Alice, but I didn't want to regret calling. My dad may have been waiting by the phone or had her phone, and I couldn't risk it, at least not yet. Mulling over the night's events, I laid down and before I knew it, I was fast asleep.

Available Now On All Platforms

OTHER BOOKS BY

Charge It To The Game 2

A Summer To Remember With My Hitta

Snatched Up By A Hitta

Santa Sent Me A Real One For Christmas

Wet Dreams on Lockdown: The Unit Manager

By **Nai**

A Setup For Revenge

Wet Dreams On Lockdown: Librarian

By **Ashley Williams**

Ridin' For You

Trickin' on a Heaux for Christmas: A BBW Love Story

Homie Hoppin' For The Holidays

By **Telia Teanna**

The State's Witness

The State's Witness 2

The State's Witness 3

By **Kyiris Ashley**

Stuck In The Trenches

Stuck In The Trenches 2

By **Huff Tha Great**

The Swipe

By **Toōla**

Melted the Heart of a Menace

By P. Wise

Merry Trapmas: Ice & Frost

By **Mia Sky**

Thug Me The Right Way

By **DiamondATL & Nai**

Wet Dreams on Lockdown: The Male C.O

By **Tamyra Griffin**

Ridin For You, Too
Wet Dreams On Lockdown: The Female C.O
By **Telia Teanna**

A Setup For Revenge 2
By **Ashley Williams**

A Gangsta's Last Kiss
By **Mia Sky**

Pretti & The Beast
Wet Dreams On Lockdown: Lieutenant Grace
By **P. Wise**

Wet Dreams On Lockdown: The Captain
By **TN Jones**

Wet Dreams On Lockdown: The Warden
By **Shawnice**

BOOKS BY

URBAN AINT DEAD's C.E.O

<u>Elijah R. Freeman</u>

Triggadale

Triggadale 2

Triggadale 3

Tales 4rm Da Dale

The Hottest Summer Ever

Murda Was The Case

Murda Was The Case 2

Murda Was The Case 3

Hittin' Licks For The Holidays: Atlanta

Wet Dreams On Lockdown: The Nurse